REASONS
to
STAY

For my mother, Hazel Mays Walden
    my grandfather, Perry Burton Wood Mays
    my great-grandmother, Mary Ann Mays

Library of Congress Cataloging-in-Publication Data

Froehlich, Margaret Walden.
  Reasons to stay.

  Summary: After her mother's death, twelve-year-old
Babe begins to learn some hard truths about her
mother's life — truths that shake her confidence and her
sense of self-worth.
  [1. Mothers and daughters — Fiction. 2. Identity —
Fiction. 3. Poverty — Fiction. 4. Country life —
Fiction. 5. Family life — Fiction] I. Title.
PZ7.F9197Re 1986   [Fic]   86–10322
ISBN 0–395–41068–1

Printed in the United States of America

S 10 9 8 7 6 5 4 3 2 1

REASONS
to
STAY

Margaret Walden Froehlich

Houghton Mifflin Company
Boston 1986

Monday, October 1, 1906

Chapter 1

Mrs. Snoop Brown worked her way through weeds and brush back into Garbers' place the first day of October. She wore a bonnet against the sun and a shawl against the freshness of the morning air and she was carrying a peck basket of yellowing cucumbers. Florence let Mrs. Brown into the house before Babe could stop her.

Babe was trying to get Rivius to let her look at the bottom of his foot. He'd been hobbling since yesterday. Babe suspected that there was a splinter in his foot and that the splinter had come off the old barn wall. She'd noticed that the flood of sweet peas that grew at the barn's corner was stomped down. Oh, he'd waded in there all right. He'd grabbed on to the window sill and skinned up the barn wall with his bare feet so that he could spy on the hound Pa had cached in the barn.

Babe turned from Rivius, hooking her pale hair behind her ears. She pressed her lips tight and frowned at Florence because she had let Mrs. Brown in. Florence looked pointedly at Mrs. Brown's cucumbers. Babe sniffed. The old things weren't fit for pigs. If Florence saw her chance to take something from Mrs. Brown, she did — in spite of the fact that Pa tanned them if they had anything to do with the woman. Mama had always gone to lengths to avoid Mrs. Brown. She'd shush them and shoo them into the back room and try to make them be quiet until Mrs. Brown grew tired of rapping and hollering and left.

Rivius rolled from Babe's reach and made for the door. He sprang across the rickety porch, jumped down into the dirtyard and disappeared around the corner of the house.

"Let to run wild," Mrs. Brown grumbled. "Monkeyshines," she said. "If I know anything about it, he's old enough to be down to the schoolhouse. Isn't he nearabouts seven?"

Florence chewed the ends of her black hair and glanced at Babe.

Mrs. Brown said, "I know good and well he hasn't set the first foot down in that schoolhouse and from what my Het tells me, neither of you girls has been down there this term either. Twelve, Babe, and you almost thirteen, Florence, and if I don't miss my guess, the two of you are just lallygagging around day in and day out."

"I don't lallygag around," Babe said.

"Full of sass, too," Mrs. Brown said, looking hard at Babe. Babe stared back. Mrs. Brown's eyes were the color of acorns, she decided.

"Where's Annamae?" Mrs. Brown asked. "I didn't see her out puttering around her posies." She ducked her head to glimpse out the window. "I never see the likes of decking the way to the outhouse and barn with flowers. If I's her, I'd have devoted me to planting cabbages or cucumbers or potatoes or something since Mr. Garber ain't been working. I should think he'd be anxious to get back with the section gang—unless, of course, they'll not have him." Mrs. Brown noticed a patch of sticktights prickling along the edge of her shawl. "It wouldn't hurt him to scythe down some of the weeds around here," she said. "I know he's been back on his feet these several weeks now because I've seen him going back and forth to Crowleys'.

"Where is Annamae?"

Babe saw Florence's dark eyes flicker toward the faded curtain that hung across the doorway to the larger of the back rooms. In a loud voice Babe said, "Mama's around here someplace or other — she's around." It made her angry that Mrs. Brown never did Mama the dignity of calling her Mrs. Garber. No, it was always Annamae, as though Mama were one of the rest of them.

"Not ailing, is she?"

"No," Babe lied, "she's not. Last I saw, she was pulling suckers away from the lilac bush." Babe would have made up more to tell Mrs. Brown but the knowledge that Mama was sick in the bedroom lay heavy on her. Mama'd been scrawny of neck and arm all summer long and her belly swollen. Now, these last few days, she'd had fever and chills and had taken to her bed. She had fretted about the lilac, though. Last April its blooms had been puny and every now and then Mama would say it was due to those long, useless whips coming up at the feet of the bush — suckers, she called them. She said she'd heard tell they sapped a bush of its strength and when she could get to it, she intended to root those out of there. "This April coming up, I mean to have bouquets to my heart's content," Mama said. "Mrs. Peterson, she always . . ."

"Mrs. Peterson who?" Babe asked, but Mama just said, "Oh, never mind . . ."

When Mrs. Brown left, Babe thought she would go and try to pull some of those suckers for Mama — that was something she could do.

Mrs. Snoop Brown spoke and jarred Babe from her thoughts. "I see you staring at these cucumbers, Babe. Yellowish though they may be, there's still good in them. They make up into a awful nice pickle if somebody'll stir their stumps. Hard up as you folks are, if I's you, I wouldn't look a gift horse in the mouth."

"I wasn't looking you in the mouth," Babe said, hooking her hair behind her ears and scratching an ankle with her other foot.

Mrs. Brown gave a little snort. Then she noticed Rivius peeking in the window from the porch and she called, "Get in here, young man." She turned to Babe and ordered, "Get him in here."

Babe scratched her ankle again before she moved. She leaned out, holding the broken screen door back, and grimaced at Rivius. "You're wanted," she mouthed at him. A second later, Mrs. Brown crowded into the doorway just at the right moment to serve as the target for Rivius' spit. Babe strained to keep from laughing.

Mrs. Brown bounced out onto the porch and took hold of Rivius' ear.

"Ow!" he cried, going up on tiptoe. Still holding his ear, Mrs. Brown made him get a dock leaf to wipe the dollop of foam off her apron. Then she transferred her grip to his elbow. "Listen, have you any proper clothing?" she asked.

"Ow" was all he would say, rubbing his ear and grinning foolishly at Babe. She frowned at him. She was still aggravated over his refusal to let her look at his foot.

"Has he clothing fit for school? Have any of you anything fitten?" Mrs. Brown asked Babe.

"Oh, he's got fancy clothes — we all do," Babe said, warning Florence with one raised eyebrow not to say otherwise. "They're laid by till cold weather."

"Do tell me," Mrs. Brown said. "You've no more fancy clothes over here than the man in the moon. Lackadaisical as everything else is, I'll warrant you've no more than the shimmies on your backs to cover your nakednesses, any of you."

Babe knew they were all going to burst out laughing over the word *nakednesses*. When laughter spurted out of Rivius and Florence, she laughed, too; she couldn't help it. Mrs. Snoop Brown left, mad as a wet hen.

"Good riddance to bad rubbage," Florence said, examining a cucumber.

"The word's *rubbish,* not *rubbage,*" Babe said, "and I wouldn't eat one of those for more than a hundred dollars. You can be sure they're bitter as gall and the seeds are hard enough to crack your teeth right in two. Talk about rubbish . . ."

Toward evening, Mrs. Brown was back with school clothing for all of them. This time, Babe answered her rap. She held the door ajar with her knee braced behind it. Florence and Rivius were on the porch, wrangling over a pail of green walnuts. Babe had been boiling coffee. She had cut bread and sugared it, intending to pour coffee over it to make bruckles for supper. Mama was a one for coffee. Maybe it would make her feel better.

Mrs. Brown, with one hand on the doorjamb, had her foot poised to take the step. Babe held the door at a steady three inches. Shortly, Mrs. Brown set her foot back down on the porch. She said to Babe, through the crack, "Annamae'd ought to come out here and see what she thinks."

Florence had gotten up. Her eyes sparkled at the sight of the faded clothing draped over Mrs. Brown's arm.

"Mama's not home," Babe said. She heard breath catch in Florence's throat. Rivius looked up at her. Babe said, "Mama's gone down to Fetzers' for milk. Besides, we have clothes. Mama's sewed all fall for us. Haven't you seen me and Florence at the dry goods store for thread and that a million times?"

"If I's you, Babe," Mrs. Brown said, "I wouldn't lie so blithe. I know what goes on over here and what doesn't." Her plump hand fluttered a little on Florence's shoulder.

"Who's lying?" Babe said softly. She shook her hair loose from behind her ears to hide her face.

Mrs. Brown turned her back on Babe and said to Florence, "Let's just see what we have here." She held up a calico and the lawn pinafore that went with it. "Het's a awful easy youngster on her clothes," she said. "Now, that's becoming, if I do say so." She smoothed her daughter's dress to Florence's shoulders and stooped to see where it fell against her legs.

"It fits, don't you think?" Florence asked anxiously.

Mrs. Brown said, "Well, truth to tell, it's picked a bit quick, but it'll serve unless Babe would rather have it, her being a trifle shorter."

Babe narrowed the door opening. Mrs. Brown eyed the door for a moment and then piled the dresses on Florence's eager arms. She held up a shirt made of sacks still blued with letters. "I've saved flour sacks a'purpose," she said, "but I'll

6

never get to 'em so I've run up a shirt which'll serve for him, there. I've turned an old skirt and made it over into a pair of britches. This is a good wool serge — it'll wear like iron."

Rivius stood up. Backing away from Mrs. Brown and Florence, he stumbled and fell off the low porch. Instantly, he jumped up and began to prance backwards, favoring his left foot. He stuck out his tongue at Mrs. Brown and called, "I'm not wearing those!"

"A hairbrush had ought to be taken to both ends of that boy," Mrs. Brown muttered. She flapped the shirt and britches onto the clothing Florence held and said, "Well, as a good Free Methodist woman, I've done my duty, not that I expect it to do a particle of good." She started across the dirtyard toward the path to her house, ignoring Rivius.

"Hey, Mrs. Snoop Bro-own," he called.

A grin flickered on Babe's face as she crossed back to the stove. She set the coffeepot off, lifted the lid, and peeked at the fire. She fiddled the stove dampers shut and began to worry again. She hoped Mama would eat something this evening.

"These clothes are better than the cucumbers, don't you think, Babe?" Florence said.

"No, not much."

"You mad?"

"I don't give two pins if you take clothes from Mrs. Snoop Brown, but I'm not." Babe poured a cup of coffee for Mama and poured more coffee over a slice of bread.

"I might just as well wear them on out," Florence said.

Babe carried the bruckles and coffee into the bedroom. Her mother was lying so still that Babe's heart banged in her chest. "Mama?" she said.

At that, her mother stirred. "Ohhh," she sighed. She reached up to smooth her hair back from her face and tried to open her eyes a little wider. To Babe, it seemed as though it hurt Mama to do even that.

"I brought you some supper — bruckles and good hot coffee. Do you feel any better?"

Mama lay strengthless. At last she said, "I guess not too much is amiss. Tomorrow I'd better get up and get going." She did not offer to take the food.

"You can stay in bed tomorrow," Babe said, making room on a cluttered commode so that she could set the food within Mama's reach. "I'll manage everything."

"I know, but . . ." Mama tried to shift in the bed. "Is Mr. Garber about?" she asked.

"No," Babe said, "he's been gone all day."

"Rivius was out by the barn," Mama said. She felt along the quilt until she came across some wilted sweet peas. "He brought me these. He shouldn't go out there. Mr. Garber doesn't want . . ."

Babe knew as well as Mama that Pa kept things in the barn that he and a crony of his stole. That dog was the latest. Pa had hauled it, tied and muzzled, under canvas in the mule wagon. Rivius itched to monkey with the dog. He even made it up that Pa had brought it home to be their pet dog. When he told that to Florence, she tattled to Mama.

"Florence and I'll watch him away from the barn," Babe promised. "We'll watch him like hawks. Don't you want to eat a little, Mama?"

"By and by I will. Let it nearby." Mama drifted into sleep. There were blue circles under her eyes. Babe's throat tightened. She left the food where it was and went into the other room.

Babe lit the smoky lamp and fixed bruckles for her and Florence and Rivius. After he had eaten and licked off his plate, Rivius came to sit on the same chair with Babe. He leaned on her so hard that she had to exert herself constantly to keep from falling off.

Evenings when Mama was well, she'd sing. Often, they'd sit out on the porch long after dark set in. Mama knew a flock of ditties. When she had exhausted them, she made up some of her own, setting their names into them and rhyming them out to tell this or that that they'd done. Babe liked the true songs even better than the other ones.

The lamp wick needed trimming. Tomorrow, Babe thought, she would tend to that and scrub the chimney. If it was clean, the room wouldn't look as dim and scary. From time to time, Rivius yawned hugely until they all caught it and Babe said they should go to bed.

The three of them shared a bed in the lean-to room that had been built with lumber from the part of the barn that had caved in. Their bedstead was set close to the wall. Its ropes sagged so that the shuck tick rested almost on the floor. Rivius slept in the middle and complained about Babe and Florence rolling in on him.

Babe faced away from Rivius and covered her ear to shut out the teeth-grinding noises he made in his sleep. She wondered if Pa would come home tonight.

Babe grew cold with fear for Mama. Mama wasn't getting better. There were doctors in to Union but Pa would never stand for that. She chewed the inside of her cheek. Mrs.

Snoop Brown doctored. Once Florence had cried for two days with earache. Nothing Mama did helped. Mama finally went to Mrs. Brown and begged her to come. She came with a bottle of sweet oil and some flannel, which she told Mama to warm at the stove. Mama was so upset over Florence and so addled by Mrs. Brown that she singed the flannel. Mrs. Brown scolded to a fare-thee-well. She said Mama was nothing but a child and that she'd no business to be trying to mother anybody. She said she'd ought to go back where she came from but she supposed it was a little late for that.

Babe decided that no matter what, she would not go for Mrs. Brown. That would be a wicked thing to do to Mama. Maybe it was just a case of Mama's being tuckered out. It stood to reason that she was worn to a nub. Pa had been hurt in July when he was thrown from one of the handcars the section gang used. He kept to the house for days with a bad knee, growing more and more ornery. Rivius' monkeyshines goaded him the worst. When he was well enough to hobble out into the dirtyard, he tore the hazel bush to pieces getting switches. Mama tried her best to keep Rivius out of mischief but it was impossible. Maybe what Mrs. Snoop Brown had said was right. Maybe they should go down to the schoolhouse. Maybe a good rest was all that was needed to cure Mama. Babe began to make plans for her and Rivius and Florence to go to school in the morning.

Tuesday, October 2, 1906

Chapter 2

Several times during the night, Babe got up and stood in the darkness in Mama's room, listening to her rapid, shallow breathing. Mama was so sick that Babe thought her plan for them to go to school was next to useless. Nevertheless, when she heard birds begin to chirp in the basswood at the corner of the house, she got up to start a fire in the cookstove. She filled the coffeepot and set it and the heavy iron skillet on to heat.

When Babe came back from the outhouse, Florence was up. She had spread the three dresses of Het's in a row at the bottom of the bed. "Do you think I should wear one?" she asked Babe.

"Suit yourself," Babe said. Then it occurred to her that wearing one of the dresses might put Florence in a pleasant frame of mind and would take away one of her excuses for not going to school. Florence seldom went. If Mama brought up the subject of school, Florence cried. Pa sided with Florence. He said that school was just so much damfoolishness, that Florence wasn't Mama's never-mind anyway, and to let her be.

Babe went to school every year as long as the weather held. There was always the chance that her friend Iva Reese would be there. Once Babe had confided to Mama that she would rather have Iva for a sister than Florence. "Oh, Babe," Mama said. "Florence . . ." but she didn't finish.

The first day Babe had ever gone to school, she had been out in the schoolyard at recess and one of the big girls had strung all the children together in a ring. Then she sang a song. Iva Reese was in the center of the ring and when the big girl sang, "Point to the very one that you like best," Iva pointed to Babe.

One afternoon, when they were no more than six or seven, Babe had gone home from school with Iva. They held hands and walked the two miles in the opposite direction from Garbers'. It wasn't until Babe saw Iva's father that she happened to wonder what Mama might think about her going to Iva's instead of coming home. Iva's father was a crippled man. He sat in a chair that had wheels like a buggy and had a shawl over his legs. Babe hung back when she saw him but Iva said, "What are you waiting for? Come on in." She hugged and kissed her father and said to him, "See? This is Babe Garber from school. She's my best friend."

Mr. Reese said, "Ma, get Ivie and this little girl friend of hers a pretty apple out of the barrel." Iva's mother got two red apples and gave them to the girls. After they ate the apples, Iva took a checkerboard off a swaybacked day bed and hunted until she found a salt sack full of red and black checkers.

Still thinking about that afternoon, Babe went into the kitchen to close the damper below the firebox. Babe had never had so much fun as she'd had playing checkers with Mr. Reese and Iva. The first thing she knew, Mrs. Reese was lighting the lamp and saying that Babe had better sit to supper with them and afterwards she could sleep with Iva because it was too late to go all that way home.

The next afternoon after school, it occurred to Babe that Mama might be mad at her for not coming home the night before. When she did get home, Babe was shocked to find how upset Mama was. Babe insisted over and over again, "That's silly. I was fine. Nothing did happen to me. I just went home with my friend Iva. We played checkers."

Mama wouldn't listen while Babe began to describe how the game of checkers was played. "Oh, yes," Mama said, crying and wiping her swollen red eyes with her apron, "for all I knew, the Petersons came and took you, though I wouldn't believe Mrs. Peterson would have it in her heart to do that to me."

Babe stamped her foot. "Well, no Mrs. Peterson took me!" she said. "Nor no one else did! And I like it better down to Reeses' than I do here, so there!"

"Oh, yes . . ." Mama wept and wept.

That was the day Babe discovered that she could get up into the chestnut tree beyond the barn. It had been her private place ever since.

The skillet began to smoke and Babe set it off to the right where the stove lid was barely warm and went back into the bedroom. Florence was perched on the end of the bed, doing nothing, content in Het's dress.

As Babe was searching for her own dress, she remembered that the last time she wore it, she had torn it on Fetzers' cow pasture fence. She found it in a pile of clothing in a box in the corner and examined it. Throwing it down in disgust, she pulled an old dress of Mama's out of the box.

Rivius wakened and tried to hide the fact that their bed

was wet. Florence got up and snatched Het's dresses off the bed. "Lookit what he did," she said to Babe.

Babe made Rivius drag the bedding outside to drape it over the pump to dry. Taking the dresses, Florence went and shut herself in the outhouse.

Leaving Rivius to struggle with the bedding, Babe went inside. She peeled off her shimmy and pulled Mama's dress over her head, promising herself that it would do. I've grown this summer, she thought. Besides, twelve is the next thing to a woman — my skirt ought to reach to my ankles.

While she struggled to button the back buttons, Babe was reminded of a story Mrs. Brown told about old Corlie Wilson's grandson. He married a girl not yet fourteen. When she turned fourteen, Corlie's grandson built his wife a new outhouse for a present. Mrs. Brown told how Corlie laughed over her pipe and said, "Well, they was in need."

Babe examined the length of Mama's dress. I could be married, she told herself, but I don't want to be. She wrinkled up her nose.

"Slice bread," Babe called to Florence when she heard her come inside.

After a moment, Florence said, "There ain't any."

Babe clicked her tongue. They'd make do with the mush left over from yesterday morning.

Babe was frying slabs of mush in sputtering lard when she noticed that the bodice of the dress slumped somewhat. With one hand, she yanked on the back of it. When that failed to draw out the slump, she decided she'd keep her arms crossed over her chest at school.

Rivius came into the house. "I had a shotgun, I could go hunting with that dog. It's a hunting dog."

Florence looked up from primping and glanced at Babe.

Babe's hand flew up to wipe a speckle of grease away from her eye. "You were out to the barn, weren't you?" she said.

"Huh-uh," Rivius said. "That's Mama's dress — how come you're wearing it?"

"Because all of us are going down to the schoolhouse, that's why." If she hadn't been mad at Rivius for lying, Babe wouldn't have blurted out her plan so carelessly. To make matters worse, the golden crust from the mush stuck to the skillet as she tried to turn it. Sweat started out under her hair. Not only had she ruined the mush, she had ruined the chance of getting Florence and Rivius to go along gracefully. Babe dragged the heavy skillet off the stove and, wobble-wristed, carried it to the table. She spooned the crumbled mush onto four saucers. Mama's, she set in the warming oven.

"Listen," she said, "we'll have fun down there. They chase and they play games. Last year the teacher even let us go out wandering, looking for chestnuts. She'll probably do that this year — maybe today. Miss King doesn't give a hoot if you read or not, Florence. She'll just let you neaten up the cloak-room if you want."

"I'm not going to any dumbed old schoolhouse," Rivius said. He had taken Pa's chewing tobacco from the wash-bench under the window and was sniffing it. Babe took it without slapping him. Standing on tiptoe, she shoved it into a hidey-hole where plaster had fallen away from the wall by the chimney. She shut down all the dampers on the stove and said, "Get to the table and eat."

Rivius flopped onto the floor and began to walk his feet up the table leg. Suddenly he sat up to examine the bottom of his foot, pressing it gingerly. "Ow-oo," he said softly, squinting one eye and pulling his mouth askew.

"Now you wish you'd let me look at it yesterday, don't you?" Babe said.

"No," Rivius said. He got up and jarred Babe's hand so that a quantity of sugar fell on his mush.

As they ate, Babe said to Florence, "Mama needs peace and quiet. If we all go to school, she can sleep all day long. She won't have to do a thing. She needs rest to get well."

"What about Pa?" Florence asked. "If he comes home for his dinner, Mama will get up."

"He's got other fish to fry," Babe said, "him and Shorty Spence." She nodded in the direction of the barn.

"I'm going to watch when they take the dog," Rivius said. "I wish that dog was mine. I'm getting a dog . . ."

"Is he, Babe?" Florence asked.

Babe ignored Florence's question and got up. "While I take Mama's breakfast in," she said to Florence, "fix our dinners for school." Babe took a bowl of boiled potatoes off one end of the table and sniffed them to be sure they hadn't soured. "You can sugar these if you want," she said. She preferred salt but Rivius and Florence liked sugar. Babe knew they would eat spoonfuls of it while her back was turned. She was going to let them — maybe it would sweeten the idea of school.

The dread Babe had felt all morning rose and threatened to choke her as she ducked through the curtained doorway with the mush and coffee. She longed for a miracle to have happened and for Mama to seem better. But Mama's face was the color of feedsacks. The circles below her eyes were darker than ever and her hair was as bleak as old straw.

"I'm not going to school," Rivius said, winding the doorway curtain.

Babe nudged last night's coffee aside and placed the fresh cup on the commode. She took the cold, ugly bruckles and set the plate of warm mush on the edge of the bed. Mama half opened her eyes and sighed. Suddenly, as stiff as a jumping jack, Babe bent to brush a kiss on Mama's forehead. "We're all going to school — you can rest." She squeezed out the words and rushed from the bedroom.

No more than in the kitchen, Babe began to cry. Rivius and Florence were so struck by the sight that they followed her without balking as she picked up the dinner pail and the clothing she had bundled for Rivius.

All along Mackey Hill Road, it felt as though the top of Babe's head would split open from the effort to stop crying. She could feel Rivius and Florence staring at her and her anger at them helped finally to stop the tears. There was nothing she could think of to do but go on with her plan.

At Mackey Hill Cemetery, Babe turned off.

"I wish we was just going on an excursion," Florence said. They often came to the cemetery on excursions with their dolls. When they were eight and nine, Mama had decided that it would be useful for them to know how to sew and had set them to making dolls. Babe had complained all day about how hard sewing was but she had finished the doll and named it Jerusha. Not only did Florence not make her doll, but when Mama made it for her, she wanted to name it the same name Babe had named hers. Babe had thrown the darning egg at Florence and opened a little cut by her eye. When she saw the blood, she was so frightened and so sorry that she hugged Florence, pleading with her to name the doll

Jerusha. Mama had browned flour to lay to Florence's cut. When the bleeding stopped, Mama said, "Let bygones be bygones. Let's go on an excursion, all of us, with our children." She had carried Rivius, and Babe and Florence had carried the Jeroos, and they had gone down to the cemetery. Wild strawberries were ripe.

Up in the cemetery, Babe stripped off the shirt of Pa's that Rivius was wearing and stuck it under Silas Mathias' tilted gravestone where she and Florence kept old dishes and Florence's chewed-up Jeroo. She dressed Rivius in the clothing Mrs. Brown had brought yesterday. His dark eyes searched her face all the while. The minute the britches were buttoned to the shirt, he began to scratch.

"Quit that!" Babe said. With her fingers, she tried to make his ragged hair look neat. She spit on the tail of Mama's dress and rubbed at the dirt on his face as he struggled to pull away. "Stop scratching," she warned him.

"But these itch," he said.

The morning had a sweet autumn smell as they stood across from the schoolhouse. Usually, there were no more than sixteen or eighteen children but today it seemed more as Babe searched the schoolyard for Iva. She was relieved when she couldn't find her. With Rivius and Florence to watch, there would be no time for Iva. Iva might get hurt feelings and Babe did not want that to happen. She took a deep breath and crossed into the yard with Florence and Rivius tight behind her. They stood to wait by the black gum tree at the end of the schoolhouse. Here and there, some of its leaves had gone scarlet.

Het Brown and Susan Ellerson had to go out of their way

to idle past the Garbers. Babe's arm jerked up to thumb her
nose at them and their eyes rolled. The next moment they
ran off calling, "Ty! Tyler! Come pump for us! Please —
we're thirsty!"

Babe watched Tyler Gosse work the pump handle up and
down for all he was worth while Susan and Het squealed
their heads off as they dodged in to get water in their cupped
hands. Big Pierce Martin interrupted their drinks by stran-
gling Tyler's neck. Susan pumped then and Het caught water
to throw at Pierce until he let go of Tyler and grabbed her
and kissed her. Het's scream was bloodcurdling. Babe's face
wrinkled in disgust.

Pierce and Tyler began to wrestle in the grass as Babe el-
bowed Rivius and said, "Stop your scratching." The next
thing she knew, Het and Susan were calling, "Hey, Ty!
Tyler! Pierce!" When they had the boys' attention, Het and
Susan pointed at Babe and plucked the bosoms of their
dresses. Babe's ears burned hot as fire. The school bell rang
then and she and Florence and Rivius were last inside.

There was a new teacher this year. Last year's was a
squinty-eyed young one who knew riddles and conundrums
and cavorted around in the yard with the pupils at recess
time. The new teacher was an old woman with her hair
skinned back and bulgy shoes. Babe slid into the bench beside Florence and wished they had stayed in the cemetery
after all.

When the teacher discovered that Florence couldn't read,
she made her sit with the babies. Babe bit her lip in remorse
for having made Florence come. Florence sat, her eyes glazed,
her hair in her mouth. To make matters worse, the teacher
shut Rivius into the cloakroom because he had bitten a slate

pencil in two, chewed it, and spit it out onto the floor. There was an ominous silence from the cloakroom. Babe sat staring into the book the teacher had given her to read. She tried to catch a sound that would tell her what Rivius was doing.

At last recess came. Babe pushed past other pupils and tugged at Florence as she tried to unfold herself from the baby seat. Her dress had gotten caught in the hinge. "Don't tear it," Florence said.

"Come on," Babe whispered, working the dress loose. "Let's get out of here. We'll find Rivius and go home."

Florence stumbled to her feet and followed Babe. The cloakroom was empty and Babe was so intent on finding Rivius that she wasn't aware of the knot of pupils that waited at the bottom of the steps. Pierce grabbed her and pulled her arms behind her back and Tyler Gosse did the same with Florence.

"Come on, come on," Het urged, "get them far enough away from the schoolhouse."

Florence let herself be carted like a post. Babe relished each time her teeth struck Pierce's wristbone or each time her heels drove against his shins. He cursed in her ear and she wrenched her head around to spit in his face.

Halfway down the hollow behind the schoolhouse Het said, "That's far enough." Pierce struggled to hold Babe as Het came close and then quickly backed beyond range of Babe's feet. "You want to know what your brother did? You want to know? I ain't even allowed to say what he is, but the word's wrote low down on the privy door!"

"Bastard, Het," Pierce said, laughing. Babe tried to stomp on his foot.

Het came as close as she dared. She pursed her mouth just the way her mother did, Babe thought. Then she put her hands on her hips and said, "Your bastard brother ate my doughnut out of my lunch pail!"

"I thought you wasn't allowed to say *bastard,* Het," Tyler shouted. All of the children laughed.

"Oh, shut up, Tyler Gosse," Het said, and slapped him. He pushed Florence at Het and Pierce flung Babe at both of them. Babe would dearly have loved to fight Het. Instead, she grabbed Florence by the wrist and they headed for the road.

As she and Florence ran along Mackey Hill Road, Babe felt certain that Rivius had gone home. Her chest was tight — not from lack of breath but from dread. They were almost to the turn in the road when Babe spied Rivius running toward them. When he got close enough, Babe saw that his face was the color of whey under his freckles. His mouth opened and shut like a chicken's with gapes. She shook him and could hardly get words out of her own sticky throat. "What did you do?" she cried at last. Florence stood by, wringing her hands faster and faster.

"Tell me!" Babe screamed at him.

"I didn't do it! I didn't let Pa's dog out!"

"How could it get out when the barn has a door and the door hitches?"

"It just got out . . . Mama . . ."

Words withered in Babe's throat. She let go of Rivius and ran, leaving him and Florence on the path. She found Mama swooning near the sweet peas out by the barn. There was blood soak to her dress.

Chapter 3

Babe was up and running, her feet flying faster than her thoughts. She hardly had a notion that she was going to get Mrs. Brown before she found herself on Mrs. Brown's doorstep, beating her door with her fists.

Mrs. Brown answered, purse-lipped and frowning. Babe cried, "Mama's took bad! Oh, she's really bad. You have to come quick!"

"What is this *have to?*" Mrs. Brown asked, but all the same she took her sunbonnet from a nail and followed Babe.

Babe and Mrs. Brown managed to get Mama to the house and to her bed. Then Mrs. Brown demanded a basin of water. The drink pail was standing empty on the end of the washbench. Garbers' pump hadn't drawn water for a month. They carried water from Fetzers' spring. Babe grabbed the bucket and ran past Florence and Rivius cowering together on the porch.

On the path to Fetzers', Babe prayed that the cows wouldn't be uphill by the spring. Once when Mr. Fetzer had drawn a buggy up-pasture to wash it by the spring, Old Betsy had charged it and sheared off one of her horns in the spokes of its wheel. With blood dripping from the stump, she had bellowed mournfully. Babe had been scared of cows even before she saw that happen. She had never been able to understand Mama's interest in them. Mama thought cows friendly and playful. When they walked over to Fetzers' of an evening, she was broadly pleased if the cows frolicked.

The woods path opened near the pasture and Babe saw with relief that the cows were clustered by their water hole. The spring rose inside rock that Mr. Fetzer had built up around it. Water drizzled over the edge of the coping to form a little stream. In the lower pasture, the water collected in a depression where the cows waded in to drink.

Babe straddled the rail fence. As she jumped down into the pasture, the bucket clanged against its bail so that the cows were alerted. Old Betsy came galloping up along the fence with her tail raised like a flag.

Babe squealed and ran with the filled drink pail slopping icy water onto her legs. She got over the fence on the far side of the pasture and left Old Betsy bellowing.

When Babe got home, her mouth was as dry as cotton batting. Every breath seared her chest as she delivered the water to Mrs. Brown. Mrs. Brown hardly glanced at her. She left Babe standing in the kitchen and went back into the bedroom.

Babe watched a fly buzzing at the window and listened to Mama moan. Amongst the things on the sill was a stained bottle of Sloan's Liniment. Sometimes that was good to doctor ailments. Babe picked up the bottle and stood with it in her hand.

"There was no power on God's green earth would have saved Annamae, far gone as she was," Mrs. Brown said in low harsh tones to Pa when he came in as daylight waned. "There was more to it than the fall she took, Ris Garber," she said, her jowls quivering.

"Here, outside," she said to Babe and took her by the arm and shoved her out and shut the door. Rivius and Florence still huddled on the porch.

Soon Pa came out of the house, tall and stooped, with his broad-brimmed felt hat pulled low. He hitched up, larruped the mule, and drove away.

Wednesday, October 3, 1906

Chapter 4

The light was soft with fog when Babe woke the next morning. She could hear Florence sucking her thumb over against the wall. Rivius snored against her back. Suddenly Babe remembered that Mama was dead. She had known that yesterday, of course, but she had forgotten it in her sleep. She lay for a bit, watching the fog go frail at the window. A crow flew past. Crows always reminded her of Pa, awkward and bony and ragged. His hair was as black as a crow's feathers. He was as rascally as a crow, too. Babe got up. On her feet, she felt vastly weak.

Coming back from the outhouse, Babe tried to concentrate on things of no consequence. She noticed her own foot tracks in the dirt and thought how peculiar it was that each print had a missing place along the inside center. She meant to examine the bottoms of her feet to see if they were really like that but she forgot to do it. It seemed as though her mind wouldn't turn away from the fact that Mama had died.

Pa sat at the table for a while, though he wouldn't take any of the coffee that Mrs. Brown brought over. Nor would he take any of the skimmed milk. Mrs. Brown had carried over a kettle of soaked butter beans to cook up and their scent filled the house, thick as must. She also brought a loaf of bread and an elderberry pie which Rivius couldn't keep his eyes away from. When she wasn't looking, he would put his nose close to the pie or slyly put out his finger to pick the crust.

For the most part, Mrs. Brown bustled around the house in grim silence. She glanced now and then at Ris Garber, her mouth gathering ever more tightly. Babe had never known Pa to tolerate Mrs. Brown. She longed for him to tell her to go.

At midmorning, Mrs. Brown broke her silence and said, "Somebody has to take ahold here. There's clothing had ought to be fetched to the undertaker's. Had she a good dress a'tall?"

Pat sat looking beyond everything in the room. His face had a scalded look across his nose and cheekbones. He paid no attention to Mrs. Brown.

Mrs. Brown smacked Rivius away from the pie. "Had Annamae a decent dress that you know of?" she asked Babe and Florence. Florence shrugged and chewed her hair. She turned sideways in the chair so that her back was to Mrs. Brown.

"Babe?" Mrs. Brown asked.

"What?" Babe said.

"Pair of posts, you two girls," Mrs. Brown said. "Babe, come into the back room here and help me clear the top of that old black trunk. If there is anything, it would be in there, no doubt. As I recollect, Annamae come back in here with a trunk when you and she come." Slowly, Babe followed Mrs. Brown into the room where Mama had died.

Mrs. Brown said, "Give me a hand here. I've had my fill of redding and neatening this morning. Such housekeeping I never saw in all my born days."

The old black trunk had set in a corner of the back room for so long that the floor had gone spongy under it. Quilts lay atop it and leaned to the wall. Nested in them were a basket of windfall Baldwins and a saucerful of seeds. A snarl of cracked harness crushed some bunches of dill and coxcomb drying in a pail. Babe lifted some of the clutter and a cloud of moths fluttered from the quilts.

"Good merciful heavens!" cried Mrs. Brown, trying to smack as many moths as she could between her hands.

With the top of the trunk cleared, Babe discovered a thin, yellowed catalog caught between the trunk lid and the wall. It was crumpled and folded back upon itself. Glad to have a reason to get out from under Mrs. Brown's thumb, Babe walked over to the window to smooth out the catalog and look at it. It was Mama's seed catalog. Babe remembered Mama wrapping a fifty-cent piece and putting it into an envelope with her order. She had said, "Oh, I hope there will be some of the colors Mrs. Peterson had. If she didn't grow the prettiest sweet peas." Sometimes Babe thought Mama made up Mrs. Peterson the way she and Florence made up Mrs. Biddybody when they played at the cemetery. Mama often spoke her name but she was nobody Babe had ever come across. If she asked Mama about her, she always got the same reply — "Oh, never mind . . ."

When the flower seeds came, Mama planted them out by the barn. Babe had a sharp picture of the vines trampled and the bright salmon, pink, and purple blossoms crushed. Why did Rivius have to wade in there? Why did he have to turn that dog loose? If she had just stayed home and watched him instead of gallivanting off to school yesterday . . .

Mrs. Brown had pried up the trunk lid. She pawed through

things inside, murmuring to herself, " 'ary a thing useful. I might have known. One dress, and that too gaudy for laying away in."

Babe glanced around as Mrs. Snoop Brown held up a red paisley dress and peered down her nose at it. She heard Mrs. Brown say softly to the dress, "Well, little Annamae's got her comeuppance at last, I'd say."

The numbness that had held Babe all morning seemed to crack open. She felt a rush of hate. Was there ever such a wicked woman as Mrs. Brown!

Babe slapped the seed catalog down onto the window sill and Mrs. Brown glanced up with a startled look.

"You don't have a right to say anything about my mother," Babe said, straining the words through her teeth.

After a moment's surprise, Mrs. Brown's face fell into its familiar lines. "You needn't go high and mighty with me, young lady," she said. "Your mother wasn't such a much as you think."

Babe wanted to charge at Mrs. Brown with her fists. It was all she could do to make herself stand still. She stared into Mrs. Brown's eyes and let her own eyes fill with hate.

Mrs. Brown's look flickered away. She glimpsed into the other room and saw Rivius picking at the pie. "Rivius!" she squawked. He jumped and his elbow caught the brace that held the shelf. Its nails grated loose and the shelf tilted so that the pie slid off and landed on the floor face down.

Rivius stared at the pie, stricken. Mrs. Brown bustled past Babe, Mama's dress swinging from her hand, and began to scold. When she discovered that there was no water to clean up the mess, she was beside herself. Babe moved into the doorway, shaking with anger at Mrs. Brown for what she had said.

Mrs. Brown thumped the table and said, "I ain't one bit surprised at the turn things have taken over here, Ris Garber!"

Suddenly Pa jumped up, raring back from the table so that the chair he'd been sitting on overturned. His face was ugly with rage and his fists were clenched.

For a moment, Mrs. Brown stood her ground, bristling like a turkey gobbler. Then she snorted and laid Mama's dress on the table. "Well!" she huffed. "If that's the way you feel about it! It's clear my services ain't appreciated!"

Pa shouted, "Get out of my house!" and began to curse.

Mrs. Brown's mouth made a silent O. Then she caught her skirts so high that her shoe tops showed. She hurried out the door. In the yard, she began to run, elbowing the air to make herself go faster.

Mrs. Brown had gotten to the edge of the dirtyard when Pa caught her coffeepot from the stove and threw it into the yard after her. Through the window, Babe saw it tumble in the dirt. Coffee smell, dark and bitter, drifted into the house.

Mrs. Brown recrossed the yard and took her coffeepot. Then she shook her fist and cried, "And I want my bean kettle and my pie tin."

"Your bean kettle and pie tin can roast in hell!" Pa roared.

As soon as Mrs. Brown was out of sight, Pa slammed around the kitchen looking for a bottle not empty of whiskey. At last he found one, took it, plucked Mama's dress from the table, and left, banging the door so hard that the house shook.

Florence had gotten up from the table to stand by the window. "Mama's dress was pretty, wasn't it," she said.

Rivius squatted by the broken pie. He glanced at Babe and Florence and shifted to take his weight off his sore foot. "Um," he said, holding up a ragged piece of pie. "You want some, Babe?" She knelt and tasted a scrap of the pie. It wanted some in the way of sugar, she thought.

"It's sour but it's good," Florence remarked.

Babe could not tell whether it was the taste of the pie, or its scent, or Florence's and Rivius' mouths stained with elderberry juice that made her remember the day they had picked elderberries — her and Florence and Rivius and Mama. It had been amazing sunshiny, that day. They were going to pick a pailful of berries for supper and then they planned to stop by Fetzers' to splurge on thick cream to go with the fruit. They had been picking for a while well up the hill behind their house when Babe suddenly said, "Mama, lookit! We've been picking and picking and the bottom of the pail isn't even covered!"

Mama popped elderberries from her hand into her mouth. Then she jabbed her thumb at herself and cried, "Quit eating the supper berries! I mean you!" She had cried that to her ownself and they all thought it was the funniest thing. The rest of the afternoon they frolicked, eating berries to their hearts' content and calling to themselves and each other, "Quit eating the berries! I mean you!"

As suddenly as the memory came to Babe, it disappeared. She struggled to remember the elderberry-picking day — tried to see Mama and the rest of them — tried to hear Mama's words and laughter. All she could hear, though, were the choking sounds Mrs. Brown's butter beans made as they boiled away on the stove. She began to feel lightheaded. She gave a queer hollow sigh and almost knocked Rivius over as she rushed for the door.

"Ow, Babe!" he complained. "Why don't you watch out where you're going!"

Chapter 5

After she was sick, Babe made her way to the chestnut beyond the barn. She climbed up to lie along a sound limb, waiting for her squeamishness to pass. By and by, she sat up and slicked sweat from the sides of her face and hooked her hair behind her ears.

Mrs. Brown's remarks about Mama came into her mind. Mrs. Brown was a far wickeder woman than she had ever supposed. She wasn't someone to flirt at, making faces when her back was turned or sticking out your tongue as long as you were far enough away. Mama was right about hiding from her and Pa was right to lambaste them for egging Mrs. Brown on. Now Florence had gone and taken those dresses. It was Mrs. Brown's fault they had gone to school yesterday. If it hadn't been for her . . .

Babe leaned over to poor her stomach. Her longing for Mama was so strong that it made her stomach hurt. She groaned and maneuvered her legs so that she could stand on the branch where she was sitting. She sidestepped along to hold the trunk and then looked up through the tree to where her hidey-hole was.

Sometime long ago, the chestnut tree had been struck by lightning and fully half of it stuck up against the sky like bare bleached claws. Sometimes, to scare Mama, Babe would say, "Don't you wish we could of seen it get struck?"

"Oh, Babe!" Mama would say with a little scream. "Don't even say it!"

"April fool, Mama," Babe would say. She was as afraid of lightning and thunder as Mama was. So were Rivius and Florence. Came a storm, and they all climbed to sit on top of the table with their feet on feather pillows. Feathers kept lightning away, Mama claimed.

Rivius and Florence were even afraid of the chestnut because it had been struck. That was why Babe kept special things in a hidey-hole high in the blasted part of the tree. Sometimes they would stand below, blatting, "You're gonna get struck, Babe."

"Oh, go chase yourselves," she'd call down. It made her angry, though, that she couldn't help feeling a wisp of fear when they said that.

When Babe had her bundle out of its hole and had brushed ants off it, she was sorry. She had climbed up to get it to take her mind off Mama. It was the worst thing to do because inside the bundle were their checkers. Babe hadn't thought of it.

She and Mama were sharp as tacks at checkers. They'd idle on the porch or at the table all morning long, playing checkers — if Florence and Rivius would let them. Florence and Rivius were jealous because the checkers took up Mama's time. That's why Babe kept them up in the chestnut when she and Mama were finished. If Mama saw another minute in the evening, she'd sometimes say, "Babe, is it too late to skin out to the tree and get the checkers? I can skunk you. I feel it in my bones."

"Ho!" Babe would say. She'd get the checkers and she and Mama would bend their heads over them while Florence and Rivius dizzied around, whining.

Babe pulled Jeroo out of the bundle on her lap and as she did, several checkers tumbled down into the barn trash below the tree. Babe shook the doll violently. Then she adjusted her wadding and said, "Sorry, it's not your fault. What do I want with checkers now anyway?"

She spread the cloth open on her lap. Everything inside it was foolish, she saw — the stones with flecks in them that she had once supposed to be gold, a jagged piece of isinglass, peach pits. Babe saved the pit of every peach she sneaked off Betina Avery's trees. She thought she'd plant an orchard, maybe, sometime. There were several wishbones in the bundle, too. Florence and Rivius always wanted to wish on the bone the minute they ate the chicken off it. "It's too limber," Mama would say. "Let it dry a bit." But they would never wait. Then, for a while, Babe had been fierce about getting hold of the wishbones. She stored them up in the chestnut tree, promising, "When they're ready, I'll pass them out to whoever's turn it is."

Babe took one of the dried wishbones and locked her fingers around its handle. *I wish none of this had ever happened.* With the wish in her head, she pulled and the top of the bone shot off and fell down into the rotting lumber below. Babe dumped the other three wishbones, her rocks, and the peach pits and isinglass down into the barn trash, too. She lined up the remaining checkers on her thigh and shot them one by one with her finger cocked against her thumb.

Suddenly, she thought of the afternoon she had gone home with Iva. As she rewrapped Jeroo and tied her in the piece of cloth, she couldn't keep her mind off that fine afternoon at Iva's. It wasn't that she liked Iva's better than their place. Their place was all right. She stuck Jeroo under her arm and stood up so that she could see a corner of the house itself. Everything looked different to her today — lonesome.

At Iva's house, most likely, her mother was redding up or doing dishes or that. Her father was handy there in his chair. And Iva . . . Suddenly Babe made up her mind to go to Iva's. She wouldn't stay too long. She might tell Iva what had happened. Maybe.

Babe had tucked Jeroo back down into the hidey-hole when she heard Rivius and Florence begin to whoop for her. Her heart sank. She had forgotten about them. "Ohh," she groaned.

"I'm up here," Babe answered after a minute. They didn't hear her and went on calling, their voices filled with panic.

"I said I'm up here," Babe yelled, swinging down from the tree. She didn't want to take Florence and Rivius to Iva's. They would butt in. They would ruin everything. She might as well not go.

Florence, with Het's dress hiked to her knees, came running up the hill. Rivius was right behind her. "Wait up! I said, wait up, Florence!" he screamed.

"We were looking all over for you," Florence said, out of breath.

"I hollered I was up here," Babe said. "Only I'm going

someplace." She saw fright cross their faces. "I suppose you two have to come," she said.

They hadn't gotten halfway to Iva's when Rivius began to complain about his foot. "I should have left you home," Babe said.

"Well, my foot hurts."

"If you had let me take the splinter out, it wouldn't hurt."

Rivius ignored her, screwing his face up and saying "Ow, ow" and hopping on his good foot.

Babe's shoulders slumped as she stood frowning at him. Finally she said to Florence, "Make a seat." Babe locked the fingers of her own left hand around her right wrist. "Do like this," she said to Florence, "then hook onto my wrist."

"How?" Florence asked, fixing her hands first one way and then another until Babe herself lost all notion of the right way to make a seat. "Flor-ence!" she cried. "All right!" Babe said. "You make your part first, whichever way you're going to make it, and then I'll make my part and hook onto you."

At last they got their hands locked satisfactorily and stooped to let Rivius slide onto the seat. "Don't choke me!" Florence cried.

"Giddy-up there, mule, it looks like rain," Rivius said after they had come some distance. He wagged his legs so hard that the seat broke and they all collapsed in the road, laughing. The remainder of the journey was accomplished with Babe or Florence carrying him piggyback or with him hopping between them while they held him under his arms. If they hadn't gotten so silly, it would have been easier.

Babe stopped at the edge of Iva's yard with her back to the

house. "I'm only going to stay a minute or so," she said. "Why don't you just wait right here for me?"

Babe had hardly taken note of the fact that they weren't paying attention when a pair of hands clasped tightly over her eyes. The more she tried to tear them away, the tighter they held her.

"Guess who?" Iva cried.

"Leave off of me, Iva Reese," Babe said, laughing. "Who do you think you're fooling?"

"You, that's who," Iva said. Then she let Babe go. Babe stretched her face, blinking her eyes until they were able to see right again. Iva laughed at her.

"You aren't in school?" Iva asked.

"No," Babe said.

"Me neither. I don't like the new teacher."

"Me neither," Babe said.

"That teacher's a old pissy ant," Rivius said.

Iva's eyes crinkled shut with laughter. Rivius said pissy ant again and spit and they all laughed at him.

"He shows off," Babe said.

"Don't he though," Iva said. It gave Babe a good feeling to have Iva agree with her.

Iva linked arms with Babe. "Come on," she said, "see what I found."

"What is it?"

"I'm not telling — you'll see." Iva spoke directly to Babe, ignoring Florence and Rivius. Babe wished they would sit down by the road edge and wait for her. Instead, they followed her and Iva as they struck out across a narrow field grown up to ragwort and mullein and climbed a draw up into the woods. Rivius didn't seem to mind walking. He only bellyached when it suited him.

"See that?" Iva said, pointing to an old sycamore choked with wild grapevines. "Watch." She scrambled up the side of the draw to grab a grapevine as thick as her arm. She backed up, leaning into brush, and then took two galloping steps, drew up her knees, and sailed into space. "Yahoo-oo!" she cried as she careened back and forth.

"How do you like this for a swing?" she called down to Babe.

"Lemme try it!"

"Hold your horses. Wait a minute till the old cat dies, then you can have a turn."

"I want to try it," Florence said.

"Me too. Me next," Rivius said.

Babe shaded her eyes and watched Iva. "Hey, you're pumping yourself up more. Come on, let the cat die. I don't have all day. Gimme a turn." The next time Iva swung close enough, Babe grabbed her legs. Iva gave a loud squeal as she and Babe sprawled in the yellow and brown sycamore leaves underfoot.

"I get it! I get it!" Rivius cried, stretching to try to reach the vine.

Babe crawled up the bank on all fours and caught the swinging vine. "Watch out!" she yelled as she swung out over their heads. Below, Florence and Rivius squabbled over whose turn was next. Babe closed her eyes and swung back and forth through the mild sweet-smelling air. There wasn't going to be any way to tell Iva — not with Rivius and Florence along. If it weren't for them, by and by she and Iva would lie on their backs in the leaves, resting. Then would be the time for Babe to say, "Iva, you know something?"

"Listen," Babe heard Iva say, "it's my swing. I get to say who swings next. I might not let either of you if you're going to fight."

"Yeah," Babe called down.

Iva and Babe spent the rest of the afternoon keeping the swing from Rivius and Florence. All of them worked up such a heat that their faces were fiery red and streaked with woods dirt. They had a war with Babe and Iva on one side of the draw and Florence and Rivius on the other. Florence got burrs in her hair and began to cry. Babe knew they should go home. She clambered up to take one more swing first, but as she grabbed the vine, there was a curious looseness to it. She watched in dismay as it snaked down out of the sycamore.

Rivius lay down in the road. Babe walked on, her back and neck stiff with anger and misery. Florence blubbered along behind her.

"Babe, we could of had lemonade. Iva said so. But no, you had to go on home. And there's burrs in my hair and my dress is mud and I wouldn't be surprised if it's tore . . ."

Babe thought Rivius would get up after a while when he saw she wasn't going to come back for him, but he didn't. She had to backtrack all that way to get him. She yanked him up by the wrist and dragged him, screaming, for six or eight steps. Then she picked him up and locked her arms around him. He stank with sweat and dirt and he swore at her and spit. Babe screeched at Florence to come back and make a seat. Her throat ached to cry.

When they were in sight of their place, Rivius jumped down and began to run, Florence close behind. Babe walked slowly in along the overgrown path. Her throat still hurt but her eyes were dry. She stood a minute and watched a swallowtail at goldenrod. There was goldenrod on the windowsill in the house. The water in its jar had gone brackish. Mama said goldenrod made good winter bouquets — that and everlasting. Babe thought about the name *everlasting*. Nothing lasted forever. Yes, it did. She would feel the way she felt now forever.

Chapter 6

Babe shuffled on in through the weeds. When she came to the edge of the dirtyard, she saw that Mrs. Brown's butter-bean kettle lay on its side in the yard. An old hen stalked around it with one eye cocked.

Suddenly the silence shattered. She heard Pa curse and Rivius begin to holler. After a moment, Florence slipped through the door with Het's dresses over her arm and ran for the outhouse.

Babe struggled through the alder and sumac that ranged up the hill behind the outhouse. She skirted the building and waded the weeds around the side to rattle the outhouse door. It was latched.

"Florence," she said at the door's crack, "what about Rivius? Why didn't you bring him out?"

There was a silence and then Florence said, "I don't know. He said he wanted Mama. Pa's drunk. He slapped him."

"You should have brought him out."

"I di'n't think."

Babe went down the path to the dirtyard. The hen had begun to feast on the butter beans. Suddenly, the screen door twanged against the porch wall and the hen leaped sideways with a squawk.

Pa tried to maneuver himself and Rivius through the doorway. Every button was stripped off Rivius' shirt; he had to clutch the button-on britches to keep them from falling.

"By God, I'll get me a hazel switch," Pa said thickly. He dropped Rivius and staggered off the porch, landing in the yard with a jolt that made him fling his arms out. High, strangled weeping seized him as he struggled toward the hazel bush at the yard's edge. Rivius stood waiting on the porch.

Babe ran. She took Rivius' arm in one hand and the back of his britches in the other and half dragged him across the yard and up the hill. Pa had twisted a switch loose. He made it sing as he lashed away at the hazel bush with it. He was rip-roaring drunk.

"I got Rivius," Babe said to the outhouse door. It opened and Florence peeped out. "We're going up on the hill," Babe said.

The evening air was mild. The last of the sunlight lay in rosy shafts across the pale yellow sky. Florence sat with Het's dresses folded on her lap and worked at the burrs in her hair. Rivius hiccupped and smeared his face from time to time. Babe sat with her elbows resting on her updrawn knees.

"We'd better not go down to the house tonight," she said. Florence nodded miserably. Babe put her head down on her folded arms.

Immediately, Florence said, "Babe?"

"What? Let me be," Babe said without lifting her head. "And quit looking at me," she added.

"It's not me, it's him," Florence said.

"Huh-uh, I am not looking at her," Rivius said.

Babe jerked her head up. They were both looking at her with scared looks on their faces. She snorted and made her face as forbidding as possible. Pa had gone back inside the house. Babe could not see any way around spending the night out here.

The sky had turned to lavender and insects began to make their high, frying night noises. Once, inside the house, there was a crashing sound and then silence again.

By and by Rivius said, "There's bogies, you know."

"There isn't any such of a thing," Babe snapped. She'd heard Mama say that so many times that she said it automatically. Once, when they were small, Florence had heard a bogie. Babe remembered adding her own shrill scream to Florence's to make Mama come faster. "It's only the sandman," Mama told them, but she lingered on with her arms around them.

Rivius said, "Where's Mama? I want her."

"She's dead," Babe said, hardly opening her mouth.

Rivius launched himself at her and struck her in the back. "You're a liar, Babe!" He screamed so loudly that the night noises stopped. In the sudden quiet, an owl screeched somewhere down by the barn. Babe's skin turned to goose flesh and Rivius and Florence scrabbled close to her.

"It's a bogie," Florence whispered.

"It's an old owl," Babe whispered. All the same, her blood ran cold.

A long time later, Babe half woke. Her arm was asleep. The prickles in it hurt so that she doubted she would ever be able to move it again. Groaning, she pushed away from Florence and sat up, trying to make out where they were. At last, she rearranged Het's dresses to cover them and lay back down.

Thursday, October 4, 1906

Chapter 7

The next thing Babe knew, Pa's voice was shattering the morning.

"Florence! Babe! Rivius! Where is everybody? By God, when I call, come, or I'll know the reason why!"

Florence staggered to her feet, her eyes still glazed with sleep, her hands fighting air. Dizzily, she sat back down. Babe got up and saw that Pa had harnessed the mule and was standing in the dirtyard by the wagon. She wondered where he was going and why he wanted them.

Florence tried to pull Het's dresses out from under Rivius. He struck at her, crying, "Leave off!" With his eyes still squeezed shut, he blatted, "Ma-maaa."

The disturbance caught Pa's attention. Babe pulled Rivius to his feet. He clutched the britches and limped beside her, Florence stumbling behind them.

Babe was going to sidestep the wagon and go into the house but Pa growled, "Get into the wagon, all of you."

"I have to fix breakfast," Babe said.

"I said get into the wagon."

Babe shrugged her shoulders. Florence put the dresses into the wagon and climbed in. Babe grabbed Rivius around his waist and said, "Heist your feet." Then she pushed him up beside Florence and climbed in herself.

Once Pa was settled on the wagon seat and urging the mule out of the yard, Babe said to his back, "Where are we going?" He didn't answer her and she settled for a little bit to watch Rivius driving two caterpillars along with a stick. He hitched constantly at his britches. Soon Babe said loudly, "Well, it looks as though we're headed for Union, Florence." Mama would have said, "Babe, shh, don't pester — things will be all right."

Rivius stood up to drop one of the caterpillars into the road and when his britches fell, he swore. Babe and Florence glanced sharply at Pa but he seemed not to have heard.

"Gimme that," Babe said, pointing to a snarl of binder's twine behind Florence. "Come here," she said, beckoning to Rivius.

Babe began to bite knots out of the twine, relieved to have something to do. She had fashioned galluses to hold up Rivius' britches when Pa halted the wagon in front of Crowleys'. He ordered them out of the wagon and around back. They stumbled along a narrow wooden sidewalk past a mound of rubbish where blowflies buzzed. Behind the tavern, a striped yellow cat was playing with a mouse.

A large woman in a soiled apron came to the door and said, "Come right on in, Ris."

"Ain't they pitiful," she said as Florence and Babe and Rivius filed into the cluttered kitchen. Flies stuck to a curl of flypaper. Garbage worked in a pail by the door. Sausages sizzled on the stove and the air was sweet with the smells of biscuits and coffee.

Pa sat in a scarred Morris chair by the stove and drank whiskey from a jelly glass that Mabel Crowley handed to him. His round close-set eyes were red and tired-looking.

The rest of them sat to the table and Mrs. Crowley shoved clutter aside to make room. She dropped thick white plates into place. She served biscuits soaked in butter and the meaty sausages. There were potatoes and turnips fried in the savory sausage grease.

In spite of not wanting the food to taste so good, Babe ate as fast as Florence. Rivius stuffed his cheeks. Then he propped his elbows on the table and cradled his jaws in his hands while he chewed noisily.

"Ain't he hearty," Mrs. Crowley said, smiling. Then she seemed to remember herself and put her large hand to her mouth. When she took it away, her smile was gone.

Just then, Shorty Spence, one of Pa's cronies, stuck his head into the kitchen.

Mrs. Crowley frowned at him. "Go on with you, Shorty," she said. "Not at a time like this."

"What do you mean, Mabe — 'not at a time like this'? Me and Ris is working out a deal and I got us a rush order." Shorty winked. He looked around Mrs. Crowley's elbow at Pa and said, "Ris, I got a Mr. Welch from over toward Cambridge is interested in a hunting dog with some size and muscle to him."

"The dog's to hell and gone," Pa said tiredly and got up. Mrs. Crowley barred Shorty's way and whispered to him. Shorty's mouth twisted ruefully. "Why, I ain't heard that. Ris, that's a hell of a note. I'm sorry about Annamae."

Pa did not say anything. He jerked his thumb for them to get up from the table and Shorty faded out of the room.

Red-faced Mr. Crowley, with the spongy blue blotch disfiguring one of his cheeks, drove them to Mackey Hill Cemetery.

Two men stood smoking beside Mama's box. They took the money Mr. Crowley gave them and left.

Babe was seized with panic. It had not occurred to her that they were all going to the cemetery. She stared at a cemetery bush until it took two shapes. Desperately, she tried to fill her head with the sights and sounds of her and Florence play-partying here. *Mrs. Biddybody, come see my new green-spotted tablecloth. I got it at a great bargain down to the dry goods store. Like it? Please pass the sheep sorrels. No, you're not getting berries until you eat your sheep sorrels. My Jeroo's been bad off. She's had the measles. Florence, gimme a dock leaf to put over her eyes. She can't stand any light on them.*

Babe wanted to cover her ears against Florence's crying. Rivius plucked at her dress and said, "Where's Mama?" Pa jerked him by the arm. Then Rivius diddled from one foot to the other as though he needed to make water and Pa jerked him again.

At last Mr. Crowley said, "Well, she's gone 'where the woodbine twineth and the cock-a-doodle sitteth on the limb.' Now what'll you do, Ris?" Pa did not answer.

Chapter 8

Pa offered to take Mr. Crowley back to Union but he said no, shank's mare would do. Before he left, he took a brown paper poke out from under the wagon seat, took a bottle of whiskey from it, and gave it to Pa. Then, with his odd gait, he made his way down out of the cemetery and was gone.

Pa ordered them to get into the wagon. He slapped the reins against the mule's back. The wagon lurched out of the cemetery and they turned toward home.

Rivius scuttled around, trying to catch a grasshopper. When he caught it, he cupped it in his hands until it spit tobacco juice on him. Then he swore and threw it into the road and wiped his hands on his britches. After a bit, he began to sweep the dirt in the wagon into little piles, then sifted it over his feet.

Florence sat crying, wiping her face from time to time on the skirt of Het's dress. By and by, she examined the dress to see how badly she had smeared it.

Babe watched the dusty road ravel along beneath her dangling feet. Florence didn't care if people looked at her while she was crying. When they got home, Babe was going to ask Mama to make Florence and Rivius keep to the house and then she would go out to the chestnut where she could cry in private.

Why, Babe thought, she was as bad as Rivius with his asking after Mama! Last night he had socked her and called her a liar when she spoke the simple truth. Here, she couldn't keep track of the simple truth herself.

The mule had drifted to a halt and Pa growled at him to giddap. When Mr. Crowley had asked Pa what he was going to do now, there hadn't been any answer. There hadn't been an answer because Pa thought things would go along just as if Mama were there. Well, they wouldn't.

* * *

Babe was the first to notice the Free Methodist delegation standing on their porch. Mrs. Snoop Brown was foremost, holding her bean kettle at arm's length so that it wouldn't dirty her dress. She was wearing her silk, and bonnet to match. With her were Betina Avery and Lura Wendell, the constable's wife.

Babe's first thought was that they had come to arrest her because it was Betina Avery's peaches that she stole. She reasoned that because the constable was busy elsewhere, Mrs. Avery had brought Mrs. Wendell to stand in for her husband. Besides, Mrs. Wendell was twice as mean as the constable.

At that moment, Rivius spied the women. "Pa, lookit," he said in a hoarse whisper.

Mrs. Brown heard him and said, "Yes, well you might look, Ris Garber. We're here to have a word with you."

Pa turned his head and shoved his hat back a little. Then he spit in the dirt. Finally he swore and said, "Get off my property."

Mrs. Brown's kettle flapped. "You listen here to me, Ris Garber. Indeed we will get off your property and we'll take those misbegottens right along with us. If we'd done this years ago when your wife left you with Florence, we'd all be better off." She shook her finger. "We've put up with the go-ings-on over here these ten years and our craws are full to the hilt. And now this latest! No wonder Annamae hid out all summer with another baby on the way. No wonder the Lord didn't see fitten to let it see the light of day!"

Pain in Babe's temples leaped to her neck and shoulders and she felt dizzy with trying to understand what Mrs. Brown was saying.

54

Mrs. Wendell said, "Action had ought to been taken when Annamae come trolloping back in here with that Babe. If that ain't heathenish — calling a child Babe! It's my opinion Annamae was simply bent on finding someone to do the providing for her and hers."

Mrs. Brown pursed her mouth. "Precious poor choice she made, Lura. Ris Garber's done about as much providing as you could put in your left ear. Annamae come purporting to take care of him — down as he was, and with Florence on his hands." Mrs. Brown jabbed her finger at Pa.

Betina Avery plucked at Mrs. Wendell's sleeve and then at Mrs. Brown's. "Is there any recompense to be made here? For instance, Lura, is Alois going to take any action regarding the dog?

"Didn't you say, Bess, that it was blooded and belonged to them Beilers south of Union? The reason why I ask is, if claims is to be settled, I'd ought to be recompensed for my peaches. It's Babe there steals 'em. Why, it's to the point I can't depend on a scant bushel of fruit from my own tree. Do you know my pantry was empty of peaches before February ever rolled around? Used to was, I could count on canned peaches till June-July, when the new ones ripened. Seems to me, I'd ought to be paid!" Betina Avery glared at Babe.

Babe struggled to hide her shock over what Mrs. Brown and what Mrs. Wendell had said. The afternoon was heavy with heat. Florence had stopped sniffing. Pa and Rivius and the mule were still as statues.

Mrs. Wendell snorted. "Your peaches is the least of our worries. The issue of these children has got to be settled. Then Alois will deal with *him*.

"Florence's mother ain't been heard from in years — didn't

take care of Florence when she had her — no use expecting otherwise at this late date. Did Annamae ever give a inkling of where she come from, Bess?"

Mrs. Brown said, "Not that I was ever able to detect. Far as I know, Babe's just as come-by-chance as Rivius. All I know is, Annamae come trailing in here with Babe when Babe was about two. Little Annamae overstayed herself if I know anything about it.

"Far as I can see, the County Home is the only place they all of them can be dealt with and conquered and if Alois gets a move on, Ris Garber will get his just deserts as well."

Mrs. Wendell bristled. "Bessie, Alois is a busy man. He'll get here when he gets here."

Without warning, the bottle of whiskey flew through the air and smashed against the edge of the porch, spattering Mrs. Brown's silk with glass and whiskey.

"Blam," Rivius said softly below the women's screams.

Chapter 9

If it takes the law, Ris Garber, it'll take the law!" Mrs. Brown cried. "You'll get your comeuppance, same as Annamae got hers, see if you don't." She hurried after Mrs. Wendell and Mrs. Avery, who were well ahead of her on the path toward her house.

A storm of cursing came from Pa as he jerked the mule around. One wheel of the wagon got hung up in bramble and he waded in to try to free it.

Babe jumped out of the wagon and Rivius and Florence

scuttled after. The remarks Mrs. Brown and Mrs. Wendell had made were jangling in her head. She couldn't understand any of it. She pushed Rivius and Florence away from her and yanked at Pa's overalls.

"What did Mrs. Snoop and Mrs. Wendell say? Who am I?" she cried when he turned to glare at her.

Instead of answering, he swore at the mule and strained to push the wagon back out of the weeds. Babe grabbed his arm and cried, "I want to know who I am! I want to know about Mama! I want to know what happened!"

He grunted and slapped her. Past the sting of it, she yelled, "You're not even my father I don't think!"

All the while he was shaking her, bewilderment roiled inside Babe. At last, puffing, he said, "You get yourself and Florence and Rivius inside and you gather up the household truck and load it into this wagon. We're pulling out of this godforsaken place." The mule brayed loudly.

"*No!*" Babe screamed. "*I won't!* If you don't tell me what I have to know, I'm going to Mrs. Snoop Brown!"

They said Mama was a shameful person. All the while Pa was whipping Babe, she was trying to crowd that thought into the deepest place inside her head.

At last, Pa took her by the arm and yanked her toward the porch. Rivius and Florence turned and scrambled for the door. Babe held the muscles of her belly tight and made her breath shallow so that she couldn't cry. He would not make her do that. He pulled her onto the porch and thrust her into the kitchen. The minute he was outside, she slammed the door on him but he did not turn around.

Babe went into the bedroom where Mama had died so that Rivius and Florence couldn't see her. She sat on a chair around the corner from the doorway and looked at her hands. There was a three-cornered tear across her knuckle. Looking at it made it sting.

A *come-by-chance* was a baby born when its parents weren't married — anybody knew that. If Babe was what Mrs. Brown had said, then Mama was the kind of person Deborah Roe was. Deborah had borned a baby by herself out in somebody's barn and then just left it. Mrs. Brown claimed she, Babe, was *come-by-chance*. There was another word for it, wrote low down on the privy door. Het had said right when she called Rivius that. Babe's ears flamed and her heart beat in the side of her neck.

Babe heard Rivius and Florence scuffling in the doorway. Suddenly Florence pushed Rivius into the room. He called out, "Quit it, Florence!" and then stood staring at Babe.

"Florence pushed me," he said.

Florence sidled into the room. "He pushed me first," she said, looking at Babe with frightened eyes.

"I did not."

"He did so, Babe."

Babe stood up, turning a little from them so that they couldn't see her face. "You're going to get lambasted if you don't get going on what Pa . . ."

Babe's voice petered out. Mrs. Brown said he wasn't her father. She told that Mama already had her when she came in here. Mama had come on the lookout for someone to take care of her and . . . Babe clamped her teeth together. She would never forgive Mama for what she did. She would hate her and Mr. Garber. Not ever, *never,* would she call him Pa again. Not for more than hundred dollars. She would rather be dead.

58

Babe spun around. "Get going," she said. "Load up the stuff the way Mr. Garber said." The name tasted like brass in her mouth. She could hear Mama calling him *Mr. Garber* just as clear. Oh yes, she called him *Mr. Garber* but she let her call him *Pa*. Babe shoved Rivius so that he fell against Florence. "I said get going!" she cried.

"I want Mama," Rivius wailed.

"I'm scairt," Florence said. "I wish Mama was here, too."

"Well, she's not. She's dead," Babe said. "She wasn't even your mama anyway. You heard Mrs. Snoop and Mrs. Wendell. She wasn't even your mama, Florence." Babe thrust her face close to Florence's. She hated herself but she wouldn't move back even when Florence's face crumpled.

"She seemed like it," Florence whispered.

Babe turned from Florence and crossed the room to Mama's trunk. In a fury, she yanked clothing out of it and threw it on the floor. She smashed a cup and stomped some dried flowers to dust. In the bottom of the trunk was a handful of letters. Babe scattered them over the floor and kicked at them. Just then, Mr. Garber grabbed her by the nape of the neck and lifted her clear off her feet.

Rivius and Florence cried all the while they loaded quilts and clothing and dishes into the wagon. Babe stalked back and forth, dry-eyed. Everything that she put into the wagon, she put in with a slam. If Mr. Garber came close enough, she ducked so that he couldn't strike her. Rivius carried the chamber pot out and set it in the wagon. When Mr. Garber discovered that he had not emptied it first, he yanked Rivius and plumped him up into the wagon onto a corn-shuck tick. He threw the chamber pot into the yard and smashed it.

When all but the broken furniture was loaded, Mr. Garber growled, "Damn to the biddies and the County Home. Damn to the constable — let him stew." He jerked his thumb for Babe and Florence to get into the wagon. Then he climbed onto the seat and larruped the mule.

Babe glanced back toward the lightning-struck chestnut. With a pang, she thought of Jeroo stuck up in there. Sometime she would cry about Jeroo. She would never cry about Mama.

Chapter 10

They jounced along for the rest of the afternoon. Every farm had its hay stacked. Corn stood dry and brittle in the sun. Ditches and banks were choked with purple ironweed and goldenrod and poke. Dust from the road powdered everything in the wagon.

Babe's head ached as she leaned against a mattress, trying to piece out the truth of what Mrs. Brown and Mrs. Wendell had said.

Rivius slept near her, breathing through his mouth. Babe eyed his teeth with distaste. Some of them were like little brown hollowed kernels of corn. Times he had toothache, Mama would rock him and sing and sing. Babe remembered a time shortly after he was born. Mrs. Snoop had been out on their porch rapping. Mama kept to the bedroom, hushing her and Florence as they cavorted on the bedstead. Mama was trying to make Rivius take her breast and suck but all he would do was roll his head and scream.

Babe shouted, "Mama, somebody's at the door." She and Florence ran for the kitchen but Mama got up and barred their way. Something in her face made them climb back up on the bed. Florence put her thumb in her mouth and Babe busied herself picking wads of batting out of the quilt. She glanced at Mama's face from time to time and decided that Mama didn't want Mrs. Brown to see Rivius because he was as ugly as a wild monkey with his shaggy black hair and a face as red and wrinkled as an old apple. She didn't blame Mama.

A few days later, when Babe and Florence went to Fetzers', Mrs. Fetzer was showing round a baby that had come with company. He was pretty as a peach. When they got home with the milk, Babe went in to tell Mama how much prettier the baby at Fetzers' was than Rivius. She found Mama changing Rivius' didies and telling him what a brave boy he was and how handsome — handsome as a prince. Wrinkling her nose, Babe kept her news to herself and went to see if Florence was getting into the milk.

Now, Babe knew why Mama hadn't wanted Mrs. Brown to see Rivius and she knew why she didn't want her to find out that another baby was on the way. Mama didn't want Mrs. Brown to find out because she wasn't married to Mr. Garber. He was married to someone else. Babe fanned herself furiously but her face still burned with shame.

For some time, Florence had been out of sight in the wagon, hidden under the table with a quilt rigged to drape down over it. Ever since they had skirted the town of Elgin, there had been rustlings under the table. Every now and then, the quilt bulged as Florence moved about. Suddenly, Rivius sat up, his eyes bleary. "Mama, I'm hungry," he complained. Then he sank back down with a groan.

Babe eyed Mr. Garber's back but there was no sign that he had heard, or cared. They hadn't had anything since the meal Mrs. Crowley had fixed them that morning. Now the sky had gone mellow and eveningish. Babe's own stomach growled as she shifted position. She tried to remember what had been put into the wagon that was worth eating. She thought with distaste of some sauerkraut in the bottom of a crock. There were a few potatoes and carrots. Suddenly, she thought of Mrs. Brown's loaf. Mr. Garber had not thrown that out. Babe had seen Florence wrapping it in a checkered cloth and putting it in a bushel basket with some other things off the washbench. The sugar sack was half full still and she had put that in the basket, too.

Rivius looked up at her. "Fix me something to eat," he said.

"I'm not your servant."

"Ba-abe," he whined.

She twisted so that her back was toward him and waited for a pinch or some other meanness. Finally she glanced around at him. He had turned on his side and drawn his knees up so that she could see the soles of his feet. When she noticed the redness around the splinter in his foot, she relented and said, "You want bread and sugar?"

He stirred and sat up.

Babe said, "Florence, is the basket with Mrs. Snoop's bread back in under there someplace?"

Rivius crawled over and flapped up the quilt. Florence was sitting cross-legged under the table with her back to them. Babe noticed the checkered cloth wadded by the table leg.

She picked it up and said carefully, "Where's Mrs. Brown's loaf of bread?" The only sounds were the *clop-clop* of the mule's hoofs and the creak of the wagon.

"Florence," Rivius said, "I'm hungry for some bread and sugar. What did you do with the bread? Tell, Florence." He gritted his teeth and twisted a pinch of Florence's dress and skin between his thumb and finger.

"Let go of me!" Florence cried and rared backwards so that she knocked Rivius against the table leg. He began to pummel her with his fists. "You ate it, di'n't you, Florence? I know you did, you big fat pig!"

Babe's stomach felt as empty as the cloth in her hand as she squatted, watching Florence and Rivius fight. Suddenly Mr. Garber pulled her backwards out of the wagon and Rivius and Florence right after her.

Rivius screeched. "Well, Florence ate up all the bread and the rest of us got none!" He spit at Florence and Mr. Garber clouted him. Then he loosened his hold on Rivius and began to spank Florence. Her feet pranced in the road and all of a sudden, she was sick.

When Florence stood up at last, pale and shivering, Mr. Garber took her arm and said, "Since you're so all-fired piggish, we'll do without till morning and then, first place we pass, you'll march yourself up and ask for enough eats to go around here." He made them all get back into the wagon. Florence crawled under the table.

The wagon began to move again and Babe sat thinking that it was just like Florence to eat a whole loaf of bread. She never knew when to stop eating. Mama tried to excuse her by saying that it was hard to get over being hungry. Babe didn't think that made much sense.

Mr. Garber was growing more and more aggravated with the mule. The animal kept drifting to the side of the road to browse. At last Mr. Garber stopped and hauled down the bars of someone's pasture gate. He drew the mule and wagon in off the road and tethered the mule to the fence.

Rivius sat up. "Where are we?" he asked.

Mr. Garber did not answer. Instead, he said to Babe, "I'm going to walk back to Elgin. You make the two of them keep to the wagon, you hear me?"

Babe looked at Mr. Garber. Because of him, she had spent last night out in the dark. Now he was going into Elgin to get whiskey and expected her to sit here watching Rivius and Florence. Well, she wasn't going to do it.

"I said, do you hear me?"

"No, I don't," Babe said coldly.

Mr. Garber put his face close to hers and said, "You hear me whether you like it or not." Then he started down the road in the direction they had come.

Babe stared after him, concentrating her hate. Suddenly a thought came to her that made her forget Mr. Garber. *She had had a father of her own, hadn't she?*

Babe set to imagining a father who was as nice as Iva's. She pictured him playing games with her and Mama and going on little excursions with them. Maybe he would have carried Babe on his shoulders and teased Mama about her affection for cows.

Puh, Babe said to herself, *if I'm not simple, making up any such of a play-party. The truth is, my own father scatted off and left Mama and me.*

Babe began to paw through things in the wagon. Watching her, Rivius said, "You're hunting the potatoes, ain't you?

Well, I'm not eating them." Babe ignored him and went on searching for her shimmy. She was not going to wear Mama's dress. Mama had wronged her.

Rivius said, "You don't even know how to peel right. You just go *zizz, zizz, zizz* and spoil the potatoes. I want Mama." When Babe didn't answer him, Rivius slid out of the wagon and went around to Florence, who was pooring the mule. "Babe stinks," he said loudly.

Babe found her shimmy wadded in the bedding from their bed. She pulled Mama's dress off and threw it from her. She wanted to be shut of everything that had to do with Mama — and that included Mr. Garber and Florence and Rivius. Why shouldn't she just run off and leave the whole caboodle?

No sooner had she thought of running away than Babe began to see the difficulty of it. She couldn't just meander along the road. That would be stupid. Mr. Garber or maybe even the constable would find her in a short time. She had to have a place to stay and she had to have food. Her mind drifted to times she had been put out with Mama over one thing or another and had holed up in the chestnut. Once she had spent a whole afternoon rigging a way to catch rainwater so that she could have her own water supply. The hidey-hole served as a larder to keep her nuts in. The lowest branch was broad enough and comfortable enough for a bed. That had been just so much foolishness, though. She had known it at the time but it didn't matter. Now it mattered. She couldn't live in a tree.

Babe drooped her shoulders to ease the crick at the base of her neck. She was going to have to find people to take her in and let her work for board and keep. And how was she going to do that in the shapeless garment that she had put on?

". . . unless Babe would rather have it, her being a trifle shorter." Mrs. Brown's words buzzed in Babe's ears. Wearing a dress of Het Brown's was the last thing she wanted to do. Three days ago she didn't want to be caught dead in one of Het's castoffs. Why couldn't it be easy to run away? Babe thought about her father. It was easy enough for him to run off.

Babe got up to see what Florence had done with the dresses. They were in a neat pile on a hummock close by Florence's ankle. Rivius was holding a handful of coarse grass close to the mule's muzzle. The mule swung his head and Florence said, "See? He doesn't want your old grass. Leave him be. He was mine and Mama's pet, not yours. We was the ones took care of him. You never gave two whoopees for him. I've seen you throw a stone."

"He was my pet mule, Florence. Ask Mama if you don't believe me."

"Oh yeah," Florence said, her voice cracking. "Oh yeah . . ."

There was a silence and in a moment Rivius came to the back of the wagon. "Get me up," he said to Babe. She sat nursing anger over the need for a dress and pulled Rivius so hard that he scraped his legs on the end of the wagon. She stiffened, waiting for him to scream and hit. Instead, he sat down and leaned against her. "Florence is crying," he said.

Babe could smell the rank scent of the mule and the green smell of the weeds he was chewing. Mama had doted on him the way she doted on cows and Florence was the same. Babe brought herself up sharply. Florence shouldn't have been like Mama because she wasn't even related. If anyone had a liking for old mules, it should have been Babe. When it came down to it, she was almost as leery of the mule as she was of Old Betsy. He was evil-tempered and unpredictable. She begrudged him every apple Mama and Florence fed him.

Babe sat jerking her bare feet back and forth. If she could just leave . . . If she didn't have to have one of the dresses . . . By rights, one of them was hers anyway — that's why Mrs. Brown brought them over. *"I don't give two pins if you take clothes from Mrs. Snoop Brown, but I'm not."*

Babe's back ached from sitting at a tilt because Rivius was pressing against her. She shoved him. He and Florence, Mama and Mr. Garber — they were all of a piece. And her own father right in with them. Who was her father anyway? Where was he from? Did he have any relatives? How come Mama had never told her about him? Oh, she was mad at Mama!

Somewhere close by, a cow bawled and Babe stiffened. What if a cow discovered them in her pasture? Or worse yet, a bull? Beyond Browns', a farmer put his bull out to pasture at night. The animal had a ring bitten into his nostrils and a chain ran from it to a heavy timber. Mrs. Brown was given to saying that if that bull didn't gore somebody to death, her name wasn't Bessie Brown. She knew of a case where a man went out to bring a bull in that was pastured in just that same way. Well, Mrs. Brown told, the man was found dead as a doornail, every stitch ripped off, and his pitchfork snapped right half in two.

Babe shuddered. "Florence," she said, "we'd better get out of this pasture." She jumped down from the wagon, leaving Rivius to keel over against the bed tick.

When Florence saw Babe, she hastily gathered Het's dresses and pulled them onto her lap, tucking and fingering them. She was still crying.

"Come on, Florence," Babe said. "Suppose these people have a bull or a cow like that danged Old Betsy. Help me get the mule and wagon out of here and put the bars back up."

Sobbing, Florence huddled over the dresses.

Babe said, "Come on . . . how about if we go back into Elgin and meet—What are you crying for, anyway?" Babe set her teeth. Mama was lucky someone was crying for her.

Babe decided that she'd take them back into Elgin and she'd park them outside of the first tavern they came to. And she would leave. If she didn't have a dress, she'd steal one off somebody's clothesline.

Her anger gave Babe courage to approach the dark bulk of the mule. She began to coax. "Come on now, there's a nice old boy. It's all right. Come on, easy now, just follow along nice and easy." Sweat trickled under her shimmy. Too late, she saw that she had tried to turn the mule too sharply. A shaft stubbed against the wagon bed and he stalled.

"Flor-ence!" Babe cried. "The least you can do is get out of the way!" Still crying, Florence stumbled to the back of the wagon and climbed in.

Groaning, Babe shoved against the mule's side, swearing at him. She could hardly stand the feel of his hide and bones. At last, she got him and the wagon out into the road. When she turned to replace the bars of the gate, the mule took it into his head to run. Babe thought she had never been so angry—both at the mule and at Florence for not trying to stop him. She stood for an instant with her fists clenched and her eyes squeezed shut. Her breath wanted to burst out through her ears. Then she began to run.

Babe was still far behind the wagon when, suddenly, the mule veered sharply right and the wagon halted in weeds. The stench of skunk filled the air.

Rivius and Florence were coughing and crying, "Pew! Pew!" when Babe came up to the wagon. She did not trust herself to speak to them. Even in the gathering darkness, she could tell that one rear wheel of the wagon had dropped into a ditch. Hiding her nose against her wrist, she got down and tried to feel under the wagon bed. The axle rested on a hummock. The wagon was stuck. Babe lay on her back in the dank weeds and levered one foot against the wagon box. She strained and strained until her stomach felt as though it would split. The wagon did not budge.

"Babe?" they both said from the wagon. Babe sat up and cupped her hands over her ears and shut her eyes. She held her breath against the skunk smell. This was the worst thing that could have happened, she thought.

Babe sat slumped between Rivius and Florence and stared into darkness glossed with moonlight. She had a right to know what Mama hadn't told her. What was to keep her from trying to track down her own father? She wouldn't let him know who she was, wouldn't give him the satisfaction. The trouble was, she didn't have the least idea where to start.

Babe's eyes snapped open and she pulled herself up straighter. The only sound she was aware of was her own breath pumping. Then she heard a jumble of sounds and tried to sort them. The sleep noises Florence and Rivius made were familiar but . . . The sound of a strange man's voice jarred Babe wide awake.

"Brother, your rig's si'wickered, ain't it?"

"Hah, she's sound as a dollar, sound as a dollar." Babe recognized Mr. Garber's thick voice. She held her breath, listening. He and whoever was with him had great difficulty climbing onto the wagon seat.

When they were finally settled, Mr. Garber called to the mule to giddap. He and the man argued over whether the wagon was moving. At last Mr. Garber began to snore, leaving the stranger to argue with himself. "Well, the rig ain't sound as a dollar," he said. "I said she was si'wickered and sure enough she is. You can't fool old Link Roche."

Babe decided that she had been wrong in thinking that the worst that could happen had happened.

Friday, October 5, 1906

Chapter 11

The morning light, when Babe's eyes focused on it, had a flat, weary look. Heavy clouds hid any inkling of sun. In spite of her resolve to stay wide awake for the rest of the night, she could not remember when the stranger stopped talking to himself. Maybe he was gone.

Trying not to waken Florence and Rivius, Babe twisted to look behind her. Her heart sank. He was there, asleep. He had a large head and not very much hair. While she was looking at him, his eyes opened.

Babe snapped her head around and could feel him staring at her back. She wished Rivius and Florence would wake up—or even Mr. Garber, for that matter. She felt the way she did when a snake got into the house once. She had been rooted to the floor with fear. It wasn't until Rivius and Florence came in from outside that she got the courage to get the broom and lam it.

Babe sat perfectly still, her ears tuned to catch the slightest sound behind her. Even in her sleep, Florence kept her arms wrapped fast around Het's dresses. Babe bit her lip with longing for one of them.

Rivius stretched. Without opening his eyes, he called out, "Mama, the girls are hogging all the room. Make them quit!" He dug his knees into Babe's side.

Babe heard the stranger say, "No, no, Sonny, don't do

that." Her back stiffened. He hadn't any right to give Rivius orders.

Rivius got up onto his knees. He took Babe's jaw to make her look at him and said, "Who's that?"

Babe shrugged and turned far enough so that she could see the man again. His eyes were small and the color of a snake's.

Florence was awake now and Babe saw the man's look shift to Florence. "Sis," he said, "come up away from them two rapscallions. Set by me — there's more room."

He had nerve, Babe thought, to be giving them names the way he did — *Sis* and *Sonny*. Next, he'd name her something. She whispered, "Don't do it, Florence. Don't do anything he says."

"Don't pay any attention to her," the man said to Florence. "She strikes me as full of sass." Babe looked at him through narrowed eyes.

The mule had begun to jerk the wagon so that Mr. Garber awoke. He called to the mule to giddap and slapped the reins against his back until the man said, "That mule's not going to pull this wagon. I said last night she was si'-wickered and sure enough she is. One wheel's in the ditch. Here, let old Link get out and see what's to be done."

As the man picked his way across their goods, the mule kept jerking the wagon so that Link almost lost his balance. "Whoa there, Nelly," he called. He even wished a name on their mule, Babe thought, as Link put a hand on her head to steady himself. Babe made an ugly noise in her throat and ducked from under his hand.

When he had jumped out and examined the wagon, Link Roche went around to Mr. Garber and said, "You're going to need you a pry bar. Trouble is, I ain't got a lot of strength to heft. I ruptured myself doing just such, once."

When it came down to it, Mr. Garber took Florence and Babe and Rivius back with him to get the rails from the pasture gate. Florence left Het's dresses in the wagon. "Just . . . just stay there," she said to them.

They lugged the rails back to find the man going through their goods. He said, "I thought you might have something right here on hand so's to save yourselves the walk, but no, I believe you done the right thing."

Link Roche sat on the bank and watched while Mr. Garber growled directions until the pry bars were in place and the mule was able to tug the wagon free. Then, from the wagon seat, he ordered Babe and Florence and Rivius to leave the rails in the ditch and climb into the wagon. When Link saw that they were about to drive away without him, he called, "Whoa there, Nelly." Grudgingly, Mr. Garber halted the mule until the man climbed onto the seat beside him.

"I'll just ride on into Elgin, being's you're going that way," Link Roche said.

Mr. Garber pulled the mule around. "I ain't going into Elgin," he growled. "I'm bound the other direction. I'm headed for Conneaut." He pulled his black hat lower over his eyes.

"Well," Link said, "I've about had my fill of Elgin. It so happens I've connections this side of Conneaut a ways, so I'll just come along."

Babe tried to find a spot to sit. The man had ransacked their wagon so that things were more jumbled than ever. She was thinking about a time when Mr. Garber had come back from Union with just such a man as this. The man had lain in the barn for two days and Mr. Garber had gone off without him. The man came up to the house and Mama wouldn't let him in. He hung around until, with her hands shaking and dark spots of red over her cheekbones, Mama had run him off with the broomstick. Afterwards, she pushed a heavy old commode in front of the door in case he came back.

Florence was turning things in the wagon even more topsy-turvy than they were. A pail fell and struck Rivius.

"That's my sore foot, Florence!" he cried. He grabbed Florence's hair and pulled it.

"Ouch, ow," she said, rubbing her head.

"That's what you get," Rivius said. "Lookit, Babe."

Babe glanced at the foot he held up. The pail had made a little black and blue mark in the puffiness. There wasn't anything she could do about anything — not about Rivius' foot, not about their things all messed, not about the ugly man that had latched on to them. All she wanted to do was get away. She watched Florence drag Het's dresses out from under the clutter. She searched them inside and out as though she had lost something and immediately began to root around in the wagon again.

"Will you quit it?" Babe said. "You've got your dresses — now what are you looking for?"

"I had things in them I wanted to keep."

"What things?" Babe asked.

"Just things, that's all."

"I bet you had my walnuts, Florence," Rivius said.

"I didn't."

"Liar."

Babe turned away from them and knelt at the wagon's

side, watching a broad creek that they had been following for some time now. She thought about the tree back home where she could go to get away from Rivius and Florence. She tried to pretend that she was surrounded by a private space, a space that could keep them out—and Mr. Garber and Link Roche as well. Even Mama. Babe wished she could drive her thoughts away, too, and all the things that Mrs. Brown and Mrs. Wendell had said about Mama and about her. There was part of herself that she hated now because of what Mrs. Brown said.

Behind Babe, Florence and Rivius squabbled. She pressed the heels of her hands up and down against her ears to make a roaring noise.

Suddenly, Florence smashed Rivius against Babe's back. "Gimme!" Florence cried. "Babe, make him gimme!"

Babe snatched sheets of paper out of Rivius' hand. He yelled, "Babe, lookit what she did! She broke the string you fixed and now lookit—my britches fall off!"

"Babe, he took something of mine," Florence cried. "Gimme, Babe. Those are mine. I want them!" Florence tried to grab the papers away from Babe. Babe got a toehold on one of the warped side boards of the wagon and stretched her arm higher than Florence could reach.

Link Roche slewed around on the wagon seat, leaning so hard on the back that it gave with a creak. "Oops," he said, glancing at Mr. Garber. "She's not near as sound as a dollar, not near."

"And not getting any sounder, is she?" Mr. Garber growled. He glowered at Florence and Babe.

"I wouldn't have your patience," Link said. "If they's hogs, though, I'd slop 'em about now. My belly says it's dinnertime. If I's you, Garber, I'd stop someplace and send that girl up—the pretty one, not the other. Most likely, if she would ask, people'd not begrudge her any leavings that they had set by." Link singled out Florence with his yellow eyes. "You'd do that, wouldn't you, Sis? Why, I bet your belly's holler as mine." Florence shook her head.

"Now, Sis, there ain't a thing in the world to it. You just go up to a back door and if I's you, I'd put a bee in their bonnet—kind of mention that a dishpan, if they have a old one they ain't got a use for, a dishpan would be handy to set their leavings in. Tell them just odds and ends—whatever they've got set by. A dab of this and a dab of that will look so mean set in a dishpan that they'll be likely to put theirselves out to add more. I'm all but famished myself. It don't ever hurt to put a bee in a bonnet. You can't depend on people being generous, left to their own devices."

Florence's black eyes glistened with tears. She looked pleadingly at Babe.

"Don't look to that there girl for help," Link said. "People'd not give a sass-prass like her so much as a plugged nickel."

Babe sneered at him and put the sheets of paper she held into her pocket. She'd give two pins if she had left before she ever laid eyes on Link Roche.

The mule had ambled on a considerable distance before Link called out, "Now, if we ain't in luck. Sure enough that's a gristmill and where flour's cheap, there's bound to be bread and biscuits aplenty. Whoa there, Nelly. Turn in, Garber. Turn in here."

Babe watched Mr. Garber saw the reins and fight with the mule to make him turn into a rutted wagon lane. A barn

and chicken coop, woodshed and dwelling were set along
the creek bank with a high wooden sidewalk leading from
building to building and to the gristmill beyond. A railing
ran along the sidewalk. At the end of the lane stood a wagon
shed.

Mr. Garber tried to halt the mule in front of the dwelling
but the animal caught the bit in his teeth and began to run
with the wagon bouncing behind. Mr. Garber cursed.

"Whoa there, Nelly! Hold him in, Garber, hold him in!"
Link cried.

Between the wagon shed and the mill, a stout rail had
been set to warn wagons away from a sharp drop to the
tailrace below. A bag of grain lay burst at the edge of the
bank. The mule halted and tried to thrust his head under
the railing to get at the grain. Florence had begun to cry
loudly.

"Hush up," Mr. Garber said. "Go on now, the way Link
here told you to. You got a dress on. Get yourself out and
hump back up to that house and do as you're told."

"Pa, I'm scairt to," Florence wailed.

Rivius held his britches up with both hands. He was
watching Link Roche with parted lips. "That man's getting
out of the wagon, Babe," he said softly.

Babe wiped her hands along the sides of her shimmy.
When Link Roche came around and jerked Florence out
of the wagon, Babe was ready. She jumped out onto his
back, locking her arms around his throat. She had taken him
by surprise so that he lost his balance and fell backwards.
Babe tried to leap free but she slammed to the ground.

From a long way off, Babe heard Florence and Rivius

screaming. She wished they would shut up. She had the headache. Mama would get her a cold cloth and camphor.

Babe struggled to tell Mama not to splash her and swung her head, trying to get away from the water that showered her face. It woke her and she pulled herself up on her elbows. It was raining and she couldn't make out why she was lying outside in it. Her head was so dizzy that it did not seem unreasonable for a wagon wheel to be turning in the air close by.

Suddenly, the soft sounds of the raindrops magnified into shouted curses and the sounds of something breaking. Rivius shrieked and then the mule screamed. Without thinking, Babe rolled to her hands and knees and began to crawl away from the wagon. When she was on the other side of the lane, she turned and saw that the mule had broken through the guard railing and had fallen down the bank of the race in a tangle of lines.

The wagon, tilted on the bank, was making continuous breaking sounds. Rivius, half naked, clung to the side of the wagon and called Babe's name again and again. As Babe watched, he dived headfirst, his pale legs akimbo like a frog's. He scrabbled across the lane and threw himself against her.

Suddenly, a sharp handclapping rang out above the commotion. Babe saw an old woman standing on the high sidewalk. There was a green-black shawl around her shoulders. "Mister! Mister!" the woman cried to Mr. Garber and Link Roche. "Get those children away from there!" Florence was standing near the wrecked wagon, wringing her hands in a frenzy. When neither Mr. Garber nor Link made any move, the old woman took Florence by the wrist and tried to make her go up on the loading platform of the mill.

"Where's Babe? I'm scairt, I'm scairt!" Florence cried.

The old woman ushered her across the lane. When she saw Rivius, she said, "My, oh my," and pulled her shawl off to wrap around him. Rain ran down her face. The lobes of her ears were long as wattles. She had fierce blue eyes and she wanted Babe to stand up.

Babe could hear the mule thrashing. Suddenly he made the worst sound she had ever heard. She stared into the silvery rain, trying to forget it, but it echoed on and on inside her head.

Abruptly, the old woman crossed the lane. "That mule has to be shot," she snapped at Link and Mr. Garber. "Why, you've never so much as moved to cut the lines!" She climbed the steps to the mill platform and went inside. When she came back out, she was carrying a rifle. "The mule has to be shot," she said.

"Now, looky here," Mr. Garber said.

"And they call you human! If you don't do it," the old woman said, "I will."

At the moment of the shot, the rain came down in torrents. Mr. Garber faced the old woman and said, "Who's to pay me for my loss?"

"Who's to bury the dead animal lying in my son's mill-race?" she snapped.

"You've shot my mule, you bury it," Mr. Garber said and spat.

"Get!" the old woman cried. She swung the barrel of the

rifle at Mr. Garber and Link and they fled up the lane. Mr. Garber turned once and shook his fist and said, "I'll be back!"

"Be sure that you are," she said, nodding at Babe and Florence and Rivius.

Chapter 12

Babe struggled to make a quietness inside herself. She had tried to walk away from all of the trouble but the old woman had taken her by the wrist and said, "Here now." Meek as a lamb, Babe had let herself be directed up onto the sidewalk behind Rivius and Florence. Inside of her head, it was as stormy as the weather was. She was just of a mind to walk someplace quiet. By herself.

Behind Babe, the old woman had the rifle wrapped in her apron to protect it from the rain. When a dog began to bark as they neared the house, the old woman said, "That's Sprig — let me by." She edged around them and onto the porch of the house. Rapping on the door, she called, "Isobel, shut Sprig into your mama's and papa's room."

Someone inside the house shouted, "Sprig! Sprig!" and the barking redoubled. Then a voice said, "Gran'ma, he won't mind me."

"Well, he'll mind me," the old woman said grimly. She opened the door a crack and a black muzzle worked at the opening.

"Sprig, get yourself into Papa's room," she said. She opened the door further and Babe saw a terrier back reluctantly across the rag carpet. "Did you hear me?" the old woman asked and the dog turned and trotted to stand inside the doorway of a room off the front room.

The girl Isobel was about Babe's height with heavy chestnut hair done in plaits, looped up and caught with ribbons by her ears. She ran to latch the bedroom door and then stared as her grandmother ushered Rivius and Florence and Babe into the house. "Push the door to against the rain," the old woman said. Babe shut the door.

A baby got down off a rumpled daybed and ran to stand by Isobel. He wore a little tan belted dress with bloomers. There were holes in the knees of his black stockings and his legs were so fat that the top buttons of his shoes wouldn't fasten. He inched behind his sister and then peeked around at them. Both he and Isobel had round blue eyes.

"Gran'ma," Isobel said solemnly, "when you went out I didn't think it was going to be anything more than Bill Thomas scraping the railing again. I was praying you wouldn't send Little Billy up here to set till matters got squared away."

The old woman crossed to the kitchen at the back of the house and began to take corncobs out of a big basket and to throw them into the stove. Isobel stuck so close that her grandmother said, "Here, you busy yourself at this while I set water on to heat."

Rivius tugged at Babe's shimmy and pointed. The baby had begun to take cobs out of the basket and was putting them in a row on the floor. Babe pulled the shawl tighter around Rivius and made him hold it in place.

The grandmother took a towel and dried her face and

hands. Then she dabbed her hair and wiped the shoulders of her sprigged dress. "Isobel," she said, "you go upstairs and see what you can bring down in the way of clothing for the children. They're soaked through and blue as whetstones with cold." She took a tin washtub from a peg by the back door. "I'll go round to get my tub as well so that they can take their baths side by each and not so likely to catch their deaths."

Babe could hear Florence's teeth chattering. She kept her own jaws clenched and her elbows tight against her ribs. Only her kneecaps jiggled. She tried to collect her thoughts. She had been going to leave Rivius and Florence for good and run away. The thought filled her with a bewildering weakness. She stood stiffly until that goose of a girl quit staring at them and ran upstairs. When the old woman had let herself out, Babe leaned against the table.

Babe watched the preparations for the baths with apprehension. At home, they never went through such a rigmarole. If the weather was warm, they frolicked in the yard in water from the pump or the rain barrel. In winter, they daddled water from a basin.

As the old woman laid out towels and cloths and soap, she said, "I'm Mrs. Alice Shaw and these are my grandchildren, Isobel and John. I'm minding them while my son and daughter-in-law are away for the day."

There was silence, marred only by the scritch of John's corncobs against the floor. Babe let her eyes slide away from Mrs. Shaw's. She was sure the old woman was waiting for her to tell who she and Rivius and Florence were. At last

Mrs. Shaw said, "John, you've all those cobs to pick up." She shook out the nightgowns Isobel had brought downstairs and hung them from the trivet on the stovepipe to warm.

Babe did not want to tell this woman anything about them. Likely, she wanted to get in touch with a constable over the damage the mule had done. If a constable came, they would be taken back. Mrs. Brown had told what would be done with them. Babe watched her toes work the carpet. She and Mama had extraordinary long slender toes; Florence's were short and stubby.

Babe looked up and saw the old woman looking right at her. "That's Florence and he's Rivius and my name's Babe," she said softly. She thought she saw a flicker of dissatisfaction in Mrs. Shaw's eyes. Babe thought she was on the verge of asking their last name when the corncobs shifted under John's feet. He tumbled onto his back and began to cry.

"There now, see . . ." his grandmother said, picking him up and pooring his head. Isobel hurried to pick up the corncobs. The to-do the baby had caused made the old woman forget about the name. For now, anyway.

It was humiliating to bathe in front of strangers. Babe felt that what she knew about Mr. Garber and her mother and herself was hidden only by the thinness of her skin. There wasn't enough water in the tub to hide in. Babe washed grudgingly, hating everything. She had leaned forward to let the water wick soapsuds out of her hair but the old woman said no, she ought to have clean rinse water. Mrs. Shaw took a pitcherful and poured it over her head. Then, half crouched, Babe stepped out of the tub and snatched a towel to wrap herself. Her arms were still wet as she stubbed them into one of Isobel's nightgowns.

Old Mrs. Shaw made Babe and Florence stand by the stove to dry their hair. Isobel hovered nearby. She got a tortoise-shell comb and began to comb Florence's hair. "Gran'ma," she said, "could I use Mama's curling iron on Florence's hair? It wouldn't be any trouble — the stove's hot."

"We've more to worry about than curls," Mrs. Shaw said.

"You have beautiful soft fine hair," Isobel said to Florence. "My hair is regular horsehair."

"Isobel . . ." her grandmother said.

"Well, it is, Gran'ma. I can't help it. Pull a hair out of Topsy's tail and lay it side by each with one of mine and you couldn't tell the difference."

"Humph." The old woman sniffed.

"My hair won't keep curl. It's stiff and straight as a poker," Isobel said. Florence's hair glistened in the lamplight as Isobel smoothed it. "Look, doesn't she have the prettiest hair, Gran'ma?"

"It is pretty — pretty as a picture," the old woman said.

Babe remembered Link Roche's saying, "Send the pretty one." Maybe Mr. Garber would have gotten rid of him before he came back. If he hadn't, Babe hoped Florence would have enough sense to keep away from Link Roche. Anyway, she would be scared of him because he had tried to make her do what she didn't want to do and because he had pulled her out of the wagon. *There isn't anything I can do about it because I'm leaving.* Babe moved away from the stove. The heat was making her weak.

* * *

When Mrs. Shaw took Rivius by the wrist, he wound his fingers into Babe's nightgown and began to scream.

"You have to be washed," Mrs. Shaw said.

"No!" he screeched.

The old woman untangled his fingers. The shawl fell away but she could not get his shirt off. Shortly, she put him in the tub, shirt and all. He struggled so that a shower of water fell sizzling on the stove and he panted, "Babe, Babe, Babe . . ."

Sweat broke out under Babe's hair. She hated Isobel and Florence standing with their hands over their ears. She hated the old woman for being so mean. Suddenly Babe rared across the room. "He's got a sore foot if you don't know it!" she cried.

"Indeed I do know it," Mrs. Shaw said grimly. "Something's in it and festering."

Even after his bath, Rivius hiccupped with dry sobs. Mrs. Shaw dried and dressed him, rolling the sleeves of the nightgown to expose his hands and skinny wrists. Last, she held his jaw and combed his ragged hair neatly. Then she said, "I hate to when he's so wrought up but I suppose it's better to get it over with all at once. Isobel, where does your mama keep her sticking salve?"

Isobel got slowly off the daybed where she had drawn Florence to sit while she primped her hair. "I'm going to get one of my circle combs to keep your hair back away from your face." Isobel unwound some of Florence's hair from around her finger. "Oh, the curl's taking already," she said.

"Isobel," Mrs. Shaw said.

"What? I don't know, Gran'ma. Last I remember, Papa

had the salve. He jammed his finger when he was dressing the stones down to mill."

Mrs. Shaw opened a cupboard. "Oh my, Elner," she said, shaking her head. She closed the door and turned the wooden block to hold it shut. "Isobel, run round to my side and get my salve."

"Where is it, Grand'ma?" Isobel asked, crawling around behind Florence to work on the back of her hair.

"It's where it always is — in my house, everything is in its place." Mrs. Shaw began to gather wet towels and cloths.

Reluctantly, Isobel got off the daybed. "I'll be back in a second," she said to Florence. "And I'll get my circle comb when I come back."

When Isobel returned with a knob of salve wrapped in brown paper, Mrs. Shaw peeled the paper away and held the salve to the stove. "I hope this will draw the poisons out of his foot," she said. "It takes a minute for the tallow to soften."

Rivius moved around behind Babe. Babe tried to judge from the old woman's face how bad she thought his foot was. If he had let her take the splinter out when he first got it in there . . .

"My foot is not sore," Rivius said, yanking Babe to make her back away as the grandmother approached with the warm salve.

"I think you'll have to hold him," Mrs. Shaw said quietly to Babe. Babe didn't want to hold Rivius. She had already tried to deal with him.

Isobel and Florence scrambled off the daybed and Babe sank down onto it, wrapping her arms around Rivius. His screams dinned in her ears.

The old woman finished quickly. Rivius lay limp against Babe. Suddenly he struggled up and screeched, "That didn't even hurt, so there!" Then he spit on their carpet.

Babe waited for the old woman to slap him. Instead, she said, "You've a sore foot. You're a brave boy."

John came from the kitchen. His dress was soaked from playing in the tub. He stuck his tongue between his teeth and made spitting noises until slobber ran down his chin. Rivius watched him for a moment and then threw himself back against Babe, howling with laughter. Babe watched the baby showing off. Suddenly laughter spurted from her. She couldn't help it—she laughed at stupid, dumb things like that.

Everybody laughed at John and he showed off more and more until his grandmother said, "That's enough, old feather-britches. Next thing you know, you'll be crying, mark my words."

She was right. When she finally told Isobel to take John into the bedroom and put his nightie on him, he began to cry loudly.

Chapter 13

Florence and Rivius hovered close to the stove, craning to glimpse the chicken and biscuits simmering. The supper smelled so good that Babe found it hard to concentrate. She dreaded sitting down to the table with Mrs. Shaw.

The old woman would have time to ask questions. She would be bound to.

"You spread the cloth," Mrs. Shaw told Florence, guiding her and Rivius away from the stove. "Your sister can lay the plates and brother can put around the silverware. Isobel, get the salt dish and the butter."

I'm not Florence's sister, Babe thought as she set the flowered plates around the table.

As it turned out, the old woman didn't have a chance to ask anything. John was so messy about his food that she was busy wiping his hands and face and mopping up after him.

"What grades are you in? I'm in seventh," Isobel said, holding the platter of chicken for Florence to take another piece.

Florence left the drumstick she had started to take and looked at Babe with alarm.

Babe re-laced her feet in the chair rungs. "I'm in seventh," Babe said, "and she's in eighth." Then she turned to see to Rivius and get away from the subject of school.

"Why, mercy, he's tuckered out," Mrs. Shaw said. Rivius was slumped in his chair, half asleep.

"What's to be done for beds? Isobel, I think the girls can take your bed and their brother can sleep on a pallet nearby. You come round to my side and sleep on my daybed."

Isobel got up to whisper something to her grandmother and Babe thought that silly for such a big girl. Old Mrs. Shaw said, "No, Isobel, you come round my side. That little boy's had enough trouble for one day without waking up in the dark of night in some strange bed with neither chick nor child that he knows close by. He should sleep up near his sisters. You go round and get my old tied comforter. It'll make a soft warm pallet for him."

If the bed ropes hadn't been so taut, Babe could have believed that she and Florence and Rivius were at home. Rivius hadn't stayed on the pallet for a minute after the old woman and Isobel went downstairs. He crawled into Isobel's bed between Florence and Babe and slept.

Across the room, rain rattled against the window.

"Are you scared?" Florence asked.

"No," Babe said.

"Is it going to lightning?"

"No, go to sleep."

"Do you like this place?" Florence asked. When Babe didn't answer, she said, "I do. Kind of."

With Florence and Rivius both asleep, Babe tried to remember what she had been planning before the accident. She'd been going to run away from all that smacked of Mama and Mr. Garber and she wanted to find out about her own father. It might take her a day or two to land a place where she could work as a hired girl. Once she did, she could take care of herself. Then she'd put her ear to the ground. She'd ask questions to find out about her father. It was funny, nosy as Mrs. Brown was, that she didn't know all about Mama's past. There were other Snoop Browns in the world. Babe would come across one who knew about Mama and her and knew who her father was.

Saturday, October 6, 1906

Chapter 14

Smells nagged Babe awake — the smell of cold in the room and the smell of bacon frying and coffee. She slid away from Rivius and half sat, propping herself up with her elbows. Then she noticed Isobel standing at the head of the steps.

"Oh, you're awake after all," Isobel said, smiling.

Babe nodded and reached across under the featherbed to poke Rivius and Florence.

"Breakfast is all but ready," Isobel said. "Mama said I should come up and tell you. She wanted you to have a chance to eat before your papa came. I'm going to find some things for you."

A dog barked outside. Mr. Garber was already here for them. The dog was barking at him, Babe was sure of it.

"Don't worry," Isobel said, "that's only Sprig. He's barking at Jack Mason. Mr. Mason came over with his team. They had to pull your mule out of the race. I'm sorry — I didn't know all that happened yesterday until I heard Gran'ma and Papa talking. It's too bad."

Isobel began to go through dresser drawers. She found a checked shirt and a pair of brown trousers. "Aunt Caroline gave us these hand-me-downs. They're just waiting for John to grow into them. They should fit your brother." She took dresses and shoes and stockings from a cupboard and gave them to Florence and Babe.

Downstairs, the kitchen was so cozy that Babe could feel her cheeks turning red from the warmth.

Isobel's mother was a short, plump woman. She took a pancake from the griddle and added it to the stack on a platter set on the warming trivet. She smiled broadly at Babe and Florence and Rivius, wiped her hands on her apron, and then reached to tidy her hair. Hairpins were working out of it in all directions. Babe could see that Isobel got her hair from her mother. That was true in her own case, too. She had the same fine buff-colored hair that Mama had. Well, she could not help *looking* like Mama, she thought.

"Isobel's been telling me how excited she is to have girls her age for company for a change. Which is not to say that we're not tickled to have you here, too," young Mrs. Shaw said, trying to take Rivius' hand. "Come see what Gran'ma's made."

Rivius pulled his hand away and leaned against Babe.

"How's his foot, Elner?" The older Mrs. Shaw was sitting in a rocker with her head cocked to the light from the window and some sewing in her lap.

Mrs. Elner Shaw said, "Well, at the moment, his feet are hidden in Simon's stockings."

"I'll doctor it again right after breakfast," the old woman said, biting a thread. She stood up and shook out a striped jacket and plucked threads from it here and there. "Done by guess and by golly," she said. "Let's hope it fits. It's not stylish but it'll keep him warm."

"How's your foot?" she said to Rivius as she held the jacket for him to put on.

He slapped at the garment and hid his face against Babe.

Babe's shoulders were already hunched with worry over Mr. Garber's coming. Why couldn't Rivius behave and put the jacket on? He'd wish he had—Mr. Garber wouldn't care whether he froze or not.

"I think breakfast is required," old Mrs. Shaw said and took her pincushion away from John. "Let's not," she said to him and lifted him into his highchair. "Come," she said, "let's sit up to the table and eat before the children's papa comes for them. There are pancakes and syrup and bacon. I believe Simon left some fried potatoes, too—if anybody's interested. Izzy, pour milk."

Rivius perched beside Babe instead of sitting on a chair by himself. He made it impossible for her to sneak plain pancakes into the pocket of her dress. She needed to take some food along when she ran away. There was no way of knowing how long it would be before she could get settled in somewhere. Babe wished the Shaws did not have coffee. It reminded her of Mama. It made her feel sick. She tried to watch the lane from the window. If Mr. Garber came along . . . Babe glanced around the kitchen. She would duck out the back door, that's what.

"How about some more pancakes, Florence?" Mrs. Elner Shaw said, and Florence took all that were left on the plate.

"Doesn't Florence have the prettiest hair, Mama?" Isobel said.

"Wish I had it," Isobel's mother said, "not this old horsehair I'm blessed with." She laughed and went at her hairpins again.

Old Mrs. Shaw said, "Elner, you and Isobel are two of a kind if ever there were."

"Mama, believe it or not, I said the same thing last evening, didn't I, Gran'ma?" Isobel poured more milk from the pitcher into Florence's glass. "I'm giving Florence my circle comb to keep," she said. "And I want to give something to Babe and Rivius, too."

Babe wished Rivius would take an interest in Isobel's prattle. She was growing frantic over being stuck here at the table with all of them.

Isobel's grandmother placed all of the breakfast scraps on a plate. "Izzy," she said, "take these out to my chickens would you, please?"

"I'll go with you," Babe said suddenly.

"See if Duchess has given us an egg," old Mrs. Shaw said.

As Babe followed Isobel out onto the back porch, Isobel said, "Gran'ma's Duchess sometimes lays a double-yolked egg. An old lady gave Duchess to Gran'ma for taking care of her when she was sick. Gran'ma goes a lot to tend or set with people when they're ailing."

From the back porch another raised sidewalk ran to the Shaws' outhouse and the grandmother's chicken coop.

"How come your walks are so high?" Babe asked.

"Oh, every now and then French Creek floods and the race leaves its banks and we have water everywhere. This way, we walk high and dry."

A flock of white leghorns came running when Isobel opened the door of the chicken coop. She strewed the scraps for them, reserving one piece of pancake.

"Come on, Babe, we'll get Duchess' egg." Isobel led the way to the nests.

"Babe has a treat for you, Duchess," Isobel said. "Give her the pancake so she doesn't peck my arm off," Isobel told Babe. She reached under the black speckled hen to get the biggest egg Babe had ever seen.

"Want to carry it?" Isobel asked. Babe shook her head. She was wondering where she could hide if Mr. Garber came.

As they went back to the house, Isobel said, "I'm kind of glad your papa hasn't come yet. You'll have a chance to see the mill. My father is down there working and we'll show you and Florence and Rivius around."

Babe remembered how big the mill building had seemed. There would be places in there to hide.

Chapter 15

Rivius insisted on going with them to the mill even though Isobel's mother and grandmother wanted him to keep to the house. Finally Isobel's mother had buckled a pair of galoshes over his stocking feet. He did not complain about his sore foot until the door was shut behind them. Then he said to Babe, "I'm not going to walk. My foot hurts."

Down at the mill, a new pole had been set. The mule was gone but some of their belongings were still strewn along the bank and in the race, ruined.

"Lookit, Florence, I see your dresses," Rivius said, pointing.

"Ohh," Florence cried. She would have ducked under the railing but Isobel said, "Don't, Florence. I have plenty of dresses — you can have some of mine. Besides, look, some of your things are stacked in the shed. Everything isn't ruined after all."

Carrying Rivius, Babe followed Florence and Isobel into the wagon shed.

Rivius struggled and Babe put him down. "Lookit, there's one of your dresses, Florence," he said. "And lookit our lamp chimbley — it's busted."

Florence glanced at Babe before she pulled Het's pinafore out of the pile. She turned her back to Babe and began to search the garment carefully. "I knew they'd be gone," she murmured.

"What?" Rivius asked, nosing around her.

"My keepsakes," she said.

"What keepsakes?" Babe asked as Florence began to pull and poke amongst their things.

"Never mind," Florence said.

A sly look crossed Rivius' face. "Florence took the letters you threw out of Mama's trunk, Babe," he said.

"I did not! You're a liar!" Florence cried and pushed Rivius so that he sat down hard, crushing a bushel basket. He struggled to his feet, swearing and spitting. Then he began to cry.

Babe remembered the pieces of paper she had snatched from Rivius yesterday when he and Florence were quarreling in the wagon. Her hand flew to her pocket before she remembered that she wasn't wearing her shimmy now — she was wearing a dress of Isobel's.

"Why did you do it, Florence?" Babe cried.

Florence's face crumpled. "He tells lies on me all the time."

"I don't mean that! I mean why did you take the letters

of Mama's? I threw them out and I wanted them to stay out!" Babe stood glaring at Florence. She was not able to say the things that she was thinking — that Florence knew as well as she did what sort of person Mama was. Mama was *not* Florence's mother. Florence couldn't even read. She had no business . . .

"Quit looking at me!" Babe snapped at Isobel.

Isobel looked away. In a moment, she gave a tug at Florence's sleeve and said, "Let's go in the mill, okay? Papa's in there working. We'll show you around if you want and I'll give you a surprise, okay?"

Trembling with anger, Babe followed them. She did not know what else to do. Rivius had insisted on being carried again and his galoshes banged against her shins. Her blood roared in her ears so that she took no notice of the clank and screech of the turning millwheel nor of the boom of water over the dam in the distance.

"Papa's grinding," Isobel said as she let them into a large dim room. Babe could feel the wooden floor thrum under her feet as she followed Isobel and Florence to the grinding stones where Mr. Shaw was working. As they watched, he shouldered a bag of buckwheat and dumped it into a hopper. Isobel waved and smiled at him and he smiled back.

Isobel plucked Florence's sleeve. "Warm your hands," she said above the noise. She thrust her own hands into the stream of grain, warm from the grinding, that trickled from the grooved stone.

Babe glanced about. Fat bags of grain were stacked everywhere. A long row of bins held grain as well. There were three sets of millstones but only the ones where Mr. Shaw was working were turning. A sign tacked to a rafter said,

MILKY WAY

DAIRY RATION

MAKES MILK WEIGH

Isobel's father was very tall and had the same blue eyes that old Mrs. Shaw had. Dust lined the little creases by his nose and every crinkle of his clothing and his shoes.

Babe hiked Rivius higher. She thought about the letters of Mama's. Surely they had been washed away in the race — except for the one Babe had stuffed into the pocket of her shimmy. She began to wonder what Isobel's grandmother had done with their clothes. Maybe she had thrown them out.

Mr. Shaw unhooked a full bag of grain from a spout and tied an empty bag in its place. Then he shut off the machinery. There was a clear, cold silence in the mill. Isobel broke it, saying, "Papa, Florence and Rivius and Babe want to see the mill. Their papa hasn't come yet. I told Florence I have a surprise for them. Can you guess . . ." She motioned to her father to lean down and she whispered something to him.

Florence was always a one for whispering the way Isobel did. Babe thought it was babyish.

"Lookit," Rivius said against the side of Babe's face. He yanked on her neck until she looked around and saw the terrier Sprig. He had been asleep on a stack of bagged grain that reached almost to the rafters. After stretching and yawning, he came down off the bags as though he were coming down stairs.

Sprig followed close at Mr. Shaw's heels as he and Isobel

led them around the mill. Babe tried to make Rivius get down but he would not set his feet on the floor. Any other time, he would be sassing her and calling her names as he tried to yank loose.

Isobel pulled Florence over to a row of bins. "Here, try some of this," she said, trickling bran into Florence's hand.

Mr. Shaw dipped into one of the bins. "Middlings is even better," he said. "It's ground wheat with part of the bran left in." He tried to give some to Rivius but Rivius tucked his hands out of sight and hid his face. Mr. Shaw gave the middlings to Babe. She liked the sweet nutlike taste.

In a dark corner of the mill, set into the floor, Mr. Shaw showed them the cob-crusher. "Those steel knives cut the corn, cobs and all, before it goes to the burrs to be ground into cow feed," he said. "It's a devilish contraption."

When they were on the second floor of the mill and Mr. Shaw was explaining that flour was sifted through the two long drums covered with fine silk bolting cloth, Florence whispered to Babe, "What do you think the surprise is?" Babe frowned at her.

Isobel said, "Papa, we'd better go down. I promised them a surprise, remember?"

As they went down the steps, Mr. Shaw said, "Maybe they'd like to take a look down through the trap doors at the workings underneath the mill."

"It's just belts and shafts and water and cobwebs down there," Isobel said. "Let's go in by the stove and get warm."

Before they went into the office where the stove was, Isobel offered them raw wheat from a scoop. "Take some," she said. "When you chew it, it turns into gum. You'll be surprised, won't they, Papa?"

The office was off the main body of the mill. It had two windows — one facing down the tailrace and the other facing the road in front. Babe saw with relief that the road was empty — no sign of Mr. Garber.

Turning from the sunlight outside, Babe's eyes took a minute to adjust to the dim light in the office. Tools were ranged all around the walls. There was a sloping wall desk and beside it a large Hartford Insurance Company calendar saying OCTOBER 1906. Babe stared at the stark black figures. She did not see how she could get through the month of October. It went on forever.

Mr. Shaw had turned to a large map of Pennsylvania hanging on the wall above a table. He picked up a yardstick and pointed to the upper left corner of the map. "Right there's Mill Village where we live. There's our creek — French Creek. It empties into the Allegheny. Isobel's mama was born and raised in Waterford," Mr. Shaw said, pointing, "and I was born in Erie. Moved away to Mill Village, though, when I was still in petticoats, so Grand'ma tells."

And I was moved away from someplace when I was two, Babe thought, *but there's nobody to jab a map for me and say, "There, that's where you came from. You belong there — not at Garbers' down below Union."*

"Where are you from?" Mr. Shaw was asking.

Babe put Rivius down, pretending she had not heard the question. To her surprise, Rivius didn't complain. Instead, he went over to a chair where the dog was curled up on a feedsack.

"I have a dog," Rivius said. "He's shaggy, not smooth. He's a big hunting dog — a lot bigger than your dog." Babe's breath caught to hear him telling about the dog Mr. Garber and Shorty Spence stole.

Rivius knelt beside the chair and tickled the dog's chest a little. Sprig wagged his stumpy tail and Mr. Shaw said, "Old Sprig likes you."

"What kind of dog is this?" Rivius asked.

"He's a rat terrier."

"Does he catch rats?"

"You bet he does — keeps the mill clear of 'em."

Rivius said, "I have a pet dog exactly like this one and he catches rats, too."

Sprig got down from the chair and began to climb a stack of bagged grain. "I could climb up that," Rivius said.

"Go ahead," Mr. Shaw told him.

Rivius looked at Babe and said, "Want to, Babe?" When he asked Florence, she shook her head. She was chewing her gum noisily.

Babe looked out the window. She didn't know how she was going to get away from Rivius and Florence and Isobel before Mr. Garber came back.

Chapter 16

When they got back to the house, Isobel's mother and grandmother were fixing dinner. Brown loaves lay cooling on the kitchen cabinet. Corn and potatoes cooked on the stove and made the room warm with steam.

Babe sat where she could watch the lane from the window in the front room. Rivius had smeared the steam away from it as high as he could reach. Isobel was showing Florence some lace scraps she had.

Babe was thinking about Florence's having taken Mama's letters and of how angry she was over it. *I'm done with Mama for good and all but even so, I don't want Florence to have her letters for keepsakes . . . Well, she doesn't . . . They're gone . . .* Babe looked around the room. She couldn't imagine a person as tidy as old Mrs. Shaw having saved the clothing they were wearing.

Old Mrs. Shaw was grating cabbage at the table. Rivius limped across the room to stand watching. "Is that sharp?" he asked, pointing to the slaw cutter. "My mama doesn't cut up a cabbage like that. She takes a knife and she chops like this." Rivius picked up a knife.

"No, no, no," Mrs. Shaw said.

"Well, she does."

"That may be so, but I'm afraid you'll cut yourself. That's a wicked sharp knife. Where is your mama?"

Babe stopped tracing the lines of the rag carpet wtih her shoe.

"She's over to Fetzers' with the cows," Rivius said. "She'll be back."

Babe looked across at Florence. Her face had a caved-in look.

From the kitchen rocker where she was peeling apples into a pan on her lap, the younger Mrs. Shaw said, "Gran'ma, I don't know as we should pry too much."

The old woman set her mouth in a grim line and muttered, "Should that man return this minute, I think I'd be tempted to offer the business end of Simon's rifle again." She grated cabbage viciously.

Babe wanted to grab the old woman by the arms and say, "Get the rifle when he comes! Do it, why don't you!" Hmph, Babe thought, she would think I was stark raving crazy! Wouldn't she, now! Mr. Garber would come and get Florence and Rivius. There wasn't anything she could do about it — she would be gone.

Isobel had taken a Sears and Roebuck catalog off a footstool. She and Florence were trying the bits of lace on the ladies pictured in the book. "That is gorgeous," Florence said. "I wish I had it, don't you?"

Rivius bobbed his head, trying to peer under the slaw cutter. "That isn't going to all fit in that bowl," he said. Mrs. Shaw lifted the cutter and swept the cabbage around with her hand. "Umm, I love cabbage," Rivius said.

"There's a good deal left on this core yet," Mrs. Shaw said. "You can have it."

John turned from the cob basket where he had been playing and came over to Rivius. "What? Do you want a bite?" Rivius asked.

Mrs. Shaw said, "John, greedy." She smiled at Rivius and said, "It's your core — you don't have to give it to him."

"Set down," Rivius said to the baby. When John had gotten himself arranged, Rivius squatted beside him and offered him a bite of the core.

"You've a world of patience and generosity," Mrs. Shaw said as she carried the bowl of slaw out to the back porch. "The slaw can chill till the rest of the meal is ready. I'll mix up the biscuits for the cobbler, Elner — it'll only take a minute — and then the girls can set the table."

During the meal, Sprig lay under the table with his nose on Mr. Shaw's shoe. Rivius kept lifting the tablecloth to peer at the dog. He kept up a steady chatter with Mr. Shaw about rats.

"My, you're all of an interest in Sprig and his doings, aren't you," Mrs. Elner Shaw said, smiling at Rivius and handing him a slice of buttered bread.

As Rivius went to take the bread, it fell, face down, on the floor. He squirmed out of his chair and they heard him say, "Come on, Sprig, this tastes better than rats." As he climbed back up with most of his bread gone, he pulled the tablecloth and Isobel's milk spilled. Isobel gave a squeak of alarm.

"Sop it! Sop it with your napkin, Izzy!" her mother cried. Old Mrs. Shaw jumped up to get a dishtowel.

During the commotion, Babe worked bread into her pocket. She would at least have that when she left.

"Whew!" Rivius said. "That danged milk just tipped over by itself!"

"Oh, no, we don't say that," said both the Mrs. Shaws.

"It was an accident," Isobel's mother said. "And if I know anything, I'd better fix you some more bread. Between John and Sprig, you've had slim pickings."

"My dog always loves butter bread, too," Rivius said, taking the fresh slice.

"You don't have any dog," Florence said with her mouth full of potatoes.

"I do so, Florence!" Rivius screeched.

"Here, here," Mr. Shaw said, ladling gravy over the potatoes and meat on Rivius' plate. "Why don't you share Sprig with me?"

"No," Rivius said. He leaned back in his chair and folded his arms over his chest.

Mr. Shaw said, "You'd better eat up. I was wanting you to come back down to mill after dinner and help me. I'm going to dress one of the burrs."

Rivius poked his lip out. Then he said, "Florence had burrs in her hair and it was good enough for her, too."

"Oh, I don't mean that kind of burrs," Mr. Shaw said. "I mean burrstones. That's what the big grinding stones are called — burrstones. Every so often they wear too smooth and have to be roughened with a burr pick and hammer."

Rivius struck the table with his fist, making the glasses of milk jiggle. "That's how hard I can hammer," he said.

"That's why I need you to help me," Mr. Shaw said.

"Isn't he a one, Gran'ma," Mrs. Elner Shaw said, smiling.

At home, Babe thought, Mr. Garber would long since have taken a hazel switch to Rivius. She wished Rivius were Mr. Shaw's instead of Mr. Garber's. But the wish was stupid — as stupid as Florence's wishing she had lacy dresses. Babe was angry at herself for even thinking it. She'd better keep her mind on her plans for leaving.

As they were clearing the table, Isobel whispered, "Mama, could we make licklally this afternoon if their papa doesn't come right away?"

Isobel's mother said, "Why, we'd ought to make something special since we have company. You girls hurry and clear up and I'll put milk and sugar and cocoa on to cook." Isobel gave her mother a hasty kiss.

John began to draw a chair over toward the stove. His grandmother put it back by the table and picked him up. "John and I'll take some scratch out to my hens and gather the rest of the eggs," she said. "Then I've a dab of ironing— the children's things so that they'll be fresh to take along."

The gravy boat in Babe's hands dipped dangerously. "Was there . . . Did you find anything in the pocket of my shimmy?" she asked old Mrs. Shaw.

At first Mrs. Shaw looked perplexed but then she said, "Oh, yes. It's laid by up there on the clock shelf but I don't know as it'll be of much account—it was soaked through and through."

Standing on tiptoe, Babe took the wadded letter from the clock shelf in the front room and crammed it behind the bread in her pocket.

Mr. Shaw came in from the porch as Mrs. Shaw and John went out. Mr. Shaw said, "Well, Rivius, are—" but young Mrs. Shaw shushed him.

Rivius was fast asleep, kneeling by Sprig's chair with his head by the dog's haunch. Mr. Shaw stood looking at him. "Ahh, Mama, I'd have taken him down to mill but looks as though he's all played out. Should I put him on the daybed or do you want him in on our bed? How's his foot?"

"Gran'ma doctored it again this morning but it's awful sore," young Mrs. Shaw said. "I hope his papa tends to it." She wiped her eyes with her apron.

Suddenly Babe said, "I'm going out a bit. It's hot in here."

Chapter 17

Babe ran along the wooden sidewalk. She was soon at odds with its sway and had to slow to a walk. She didn't know if it was the motion of the sidewalk that made her dizzy, or her foolishness in wanting to know what was in Mama's letter, or her anger at the Shaws for thinking for a minute that Mr. Garber would tend Rivius' foot. Why, old Mrs. Shaw had run Mr. Garber off at the point of a rifle! Hadn't she told her son and his wife how she felt about Mr. Garber? Did they have to be told again?

Babe had intended to go into the mill while Mr. Shaw was still up at the house. She wanted to add some middlings to her store of food. The bread in her pocket wouldn't last her any time at all.

The letter wadded behind the bread nagged her so that she couldn't wait any longer to look at it. She had run down the steps from the mill platform and crossed to the wagon shed when she heard Mr. Shaw and Sprig on the porch at the house. Babe crouched behind the stacked things in the shed and waited as they came along the sidewalk and disappeared into the mill.

In the front of the building where the light was brightest, Babe stooped down and leaned her back in between two studs in the shed's framing. The smell of the wooden wall was sweet as she began to pick carefully, trying to separate the stuck folds of the letter. If she lost her temper, she would ruin it altogether.

The penciled writing was faded. Where the sheets of paper had been folded, they had worn to pulp and at least one line of each sheet was worn away. The bottom of the second sheet had crumbled to nothing, so that the name of the person who wrote it was missing.

Babe had to squint so that she looked up and was surprised to see how pale the sun had gone. What if it rained and here she had let a whole sunny morning and most of an afternoon go by and wasn't one iota closer to being on her way? All she'd done was to stick some bread in her pocket where it was going to crumbs while she muddled over this letter. She smoothed the pages as well as she could and then began to read, following each word with her finger.

R.F.D. 5
Waterford, Pa.
June 17, 1899

Dear Annamae,
    The weather is blamed miserable. I planned
to wash but first it rained and then was foggy
so I let it go. Pa is no difrent. You

Things would never have got better I guess you
knew. I don't want you to think I have any
truck with Petersons I don't. Most what I know
I hear from that old Lena you rember her.

*She was to William Peterson's funeral. He was
laid up to the cemetery last Friday. He took his
grief over George to his grave. Its too bad. The
flowers was awful pretty — they was from their
yard Lena said. She dont know*

*alone. Lena said she heard Dorey say if only she
had Annamae to lean on. I'll never know why
Dorey didn't stand up to William. I spose she
felt her duty was to him. Anyway it's too bad.
Would you*

Peterson. Babe read the letter again and again, trying to
piece out who the Petersons were and what they meant to
Mama and to her. They meant something and she had to
know what it was.

Babe squinted at the date on the letter, trying to figure out
how old she had been when it was written. "Five, I think,"
she whispered. "It was the year Rivius was born. Florence
was six. It was a long time ago. Who knows what's become
of these people by this time?"

Whatever's happened, I have to find out about them. Babe
studied the letter again. It was too bad there was no way of
knowing who wrote it. It had been sent from Waterford.
R.F.D. 5 didn't mean anything to her but a mailman would
know. She would have to count on the Petersons living on
the same delivery route.

Babe was on her feet. The first thing she had to find out
was where Waterford was. She wished she'd paid attention
when Mr. Shaw was telling them about his map.

As Babe let herself into the mill, there was so much noise that she decided Mr. Shaw must be running the cob-crusher. The office would be empty.

The little room was warm and dim. Babe climbed onto the table so that she could see the map better. It was a sea of dots and squiggles and lines and print. She'd begin in the upper left-hand corner — she thought that was where Mr. Shaw had been pointing. She'd go square by square.

Almost at once, Babe came across the blue line labeled FRENCH CREEK. She followed it up and down until she came to Mill Village. Then she looked for Waterford. She had to know which direction she needed to travel. Waterford was up from and to the left of Mill Village on the map. That meant . . . The sun came up in the east and went down in the west . . . Babe ducked so that she could see out the window to try to figure out what course the sun took.

Suddenly Sprig darted into the office. He sprang around the table, yapping at Babe. "Go on with you," she told him. "I'm not hurting anything. Hush yourself up and let me be."

Babe sat as far out of Sprig's reach as she could. The dog had tired of jumping at the table and barking and had gone to sleep on a heap of burlap sacks. He slept with one eye open and every time Babe made the least move, he raised his head.

The warmth from the office stove made Babe's head woozy. She was going over her plans and growing more and more bewildered. Mama didn't want her to have any truck with Petersons . . . no, with Mrs. Brown. Babe tried to make the dream untangle.

By the time Isobel and Florence discovered Babe, the day was verging on twilight. Their chatter about licklally made her head ache more than ever as she followed them along the sidewalk to the house.

Rivius was sitting on the floor with John. Spools and corncobs were strewn about. Babe wrinkled her nose at a strange odor.

"Babe, I want this off," Rivius said, holding his foot up. It was fat with wrappings and a woolen stocking was pulled over it.

"No," old Mrs. Shaw said to him. "That poultice will draw the fever from your foot. You let it be."

"I don't like it."

"Well, I know it's an aggravation but you put up with it a little longer."

"Can me and him have licklally?"

"No, supper is in the offing."

Rivius sighed and lay down on his back and began to throw corncobs toward the ceiling. John tried to lie down close to Rivius. "No," Rivius said, "you get me the cobs, I'll throw. You're no good at throwing."

At supper, Babe stuffed herself with biscuits and applesauce and ham. Rivius would only drink milk. Halfway through the meal, he slid off his chair and sat beside Babe. That made it impossible for her to add a biscuit to her pocket.

Once Rivius said to Mr. Shaw, "Is Sprig more your pet dog or is he just as much mine as yours?"

"Why, he's every bit as much yours as he is mine."

Rivius turned away from Mr. Shaw. He pushed his plate back and laid his arms on the table and laid his head on them.

Babe was angry at Mr. Shaw for leading Rivius on — pet dog, pooh. It was just pretend. It wasn't fair to tell Rivius that. It wasn't so a bit. She glanced at Rivius and cold fear replaced the anger. He was sick.

All the while she dried dishes with Florence, Babe thought about going to Waterford. It occurred to her that Mr. or Mrs. Shaw or the grandmother might know where R.F.D. 5 was but she decided not to ask. They would have questions. No, she would rely on finding the post office or a mailman. She wished she knew how far away Waterford was. She should probably take some of the biscuits set by on the cabinet.

Rivius was kneeling in front of the dog's rocker, half asleep again. Mr. Shaw tried to put him on the daybed but he cried, "Quit it!"

Mr. Shaw snapped his fingers at Sprig and patted the daybed and the dog trotted over and jumped up. Then Rivius limped across the room and flopped down beside the dog. Sprig gave a satisfied groan and closed his eyes. Rivius was asleep soon after.

Old Mrs. Shaw wiped up the stove and said, "Simon, the ashes want shaking down." Then she called to Isobel's mother, who was putting John to bed, "Elner, I'm going round now but I'll be back to doctor Rivius before he goes upstairs. He's asleep."

After Isobel had emptied the dishwater into the race, she took a string from the clock shelf and said, "Papa, play us a game, will you? Want to play cat's cradle, Florence? Want to, Babe?"

Babe was startled. She thought of Mr. Reese and Iva and felt as though Isobel were prying into her private affairs.

Mr. Shaw knew more cats' cradles than Mama by far. Three

was the most cradles Babe and Florence knew how to take off one another's fingers. Babe lost count of the ones Mr. Shaw and Isobel knew — at least seven, maybe eight. She had the bad luck to keep getting the most complicated one. No matter how hard she tried, she couldn't get the hang of it. Every time, the string slipped off her fingers in a snarl. At last she said, "I know how to play checkers. Do you have any?"

Isobel found a board but the box she took out of a dresser drawer held only a few checkers. Mr. Shaw took pennies out of his pocket to replace the missing red ones. For the missing black pieces, he sliced a corncob with his knife. Babe was anxious to tell Mama what could be used for checkers in case . . .

"Reds or blacks, corncobs or pennies?" Mr. Shaw asked Babe, smiling.

"Papa, pass the jumped checkers to Florence and me, okay?" Isobel said, settling on a chair next to Florence.

"I'll take the reds," Babe said.

Isobel began to tell the buttons on Florence's clothing and her own: "Rich man, poor man, beggar man, thief . . ." Babe leaned on her elbows with her hands over her ears so that she could concentrate.

Mr. Shaw jumped some of her men. Babe searched the board, trying to figure out all the possibilities and keeping them filed in her head. One good thing — Mr. Shaw was not letting her win. She was doing it on her own hook. When she moved her last single man into the king's row, she clapped and cried, "King me!"

"Papa," Isobel said, "there aren't any more reds to use to

make kings. You didn't jump enough of Babe's pieces."

Mr. Shaw looked rueful as Babe raised her hands in the air and clapped again. After that, her turns could not come fast enough as she marched her kings to block his last two pieces. Mrs. Shaw had to come out of the bedroom to see how badly he had lost.

Just then there was a noise at the front door and Babe was sure that it was Mr. Garber. Her mouth had gone as dry as dust when old Mrs. Shaw opened the door. She was laden with a pan of something steaming and unpleasant smelling. Flannel dangled over her arm. Babe's relief at seeing the old woman faded as she remembered about Rivius' being sick.

Chapter 18

No matter how Babe breathed, she could not get away from the smell of the linseed poultice. She was sitting on the edge of the bed, watching as Isobel and Florence gathered up clothing to take around to Isobel's grandmother's, where they were going to sleep. Babe was glad for that. It would be hard enough getting away from Rivius, let alone him and Florence both. She had made up her mind to leave at dawn. Even if the poultice didn't cure Rivius' foot, she had to leave. She had already waited too long. She glanced at Rivius as he slept. There was a pale ring around his mouth. The rest of his face was flushed.

Isobel said, "All right. I guess we have everything we need."

Suddenly Babe said, "Do you know how far it is to Waterford by any chance?"

"Why?" Isobel asked.

"Oh, I just wondered, that's all. I have connections in Waterford." The minute the words were out of her mouth, Babe thought of Link Roche. She turned her head and wiped her tongue on her sleeve as though she were trying to get a hair off it.

"Have you seen the Eagle Hotel — you know where that is?" Isobel asked. "Well, my mama was born not very far from there."

"Many's the time I've seen the Eagle Hotel," Babe lied. She wished Florence would quit looking at her. "How far is Waterford from here?" she asked again.

"Oh, maybe three or four miles, five at the most. We have walked it out past the cemetery and along the old willow road. We didn't walk back, though. Once we had ice cream at the Eagle Hotel. Mama showed us the pine tree George Washington was supposed to have climbed to spy on Fort Le Boeuf. You know the one I mean, that old pine?"

"Sure," Babe said recklessly. "I've climbed it."

"You have? I wouldn't want to. Did anybody say anything?"

"Nobody saw me."

Suddenly Florence laid the clothing she was holding down on the dresser. "I'd better sleep here," she said.

"Florence, why?" Isobel asked in surprise.

Florence shrugged and pulled a tag of her hair around to chew.

"It'll be our last night," Isobel said. "Gran'ma won't care if we talk." Isobel slumped down beside Babe.

"We might leave early," Florence said.

"I doubt if we do," Babe said. "Don't stay here on that account. Go ahead and sleep with Isobel so you can talk. Go ahead."

Isobel sighed. "I wish you didn't have to go. I wish all of you could stay forever. I'm going to be so lonesome." She sighed again. "I gave Florence my circle comb as a keepsake to remember me by. I want to give you my buttonhook, Babe." Isobel got up and began to search through dresser drawers. "If I can find it . . . Its handle is mother-of-pearl . . . Oh, here . . ." She came over and gave Babe the buttonhook. "See the rainbows? You can keep it."

Babe took the buttonhook. She felt sure that she would not see Isobel again. In the morning, she would be gone long before Isobel and Florence got up. An unexpected sadness tightened her throat. Then Babe said, "Thanks, it's really pretty. I'll remember you every time I use it."

"And I have to think of something for him," Isobel said, nodding at the mound on the bed. "Oh, I know — I have a little cast iron elephant bank. I'll fill it up with pennies. That'll tickle him, won't it? I'll dig it up when we go downstairs. You're coming, aren't you, Florence? Please?"

"Go ahead," Babe said and Florence gathered up the clothing again. She stopped once at the head of the steps and looked around at Babe, a long look, and then she followed Isobel downstairs.

It was the first time Babe believed that she was really going to go away from Rivius and Florence. She wished she hadn't lied to Florence. It was a mean way to leave.

Mama had left with a lie, too, Babe thought, turning out

the light. She counted the days since Mama's death — Tuesday, Wednesday, Thursday, Friday, and Saturday, which was about finished. She had only known about the lies for three of those days. During her whole life up until then, she had liked Mama, loved her. Now, she hated her.

Babe got into bed with her clothes on. She pressed her hand against the letter in her pocket. She wished it were from Mama. She wished there were some way to explain away the lies. Since that was impossible, she thought she'd be better served with a letter from Mama telling who these Petersons were and how to find them.

Babe felt around on the bed for Isobel's buttonhook and put that in her other pocket. Then she lay facing the window so that the first glimmer of light would waken her if she happened to fall asleep. She wouldn't, she was too keyed up. If it weren't too dark to see, she would go now.

Sunday, October 7, 1906

Chapter 19

Babe didn't know if it was Rivius' groaning that woke her or the dog's barking. Her eyes were open and it was not so dark in the room but what she could see the shapes of the furniture. She listened as Mr. Shaw whistled and called to Sprig from the back porch. She heard the door close but the dog was still barking somewhere outside.

Babe's head was muddled. When she discovered that she was dressed in her clothes, it came to her that she should be on her way to Waterford. She had slept! She turned and punched the pillow.

"Quit it," Rivius said and sat up, crying. "I want this off! I want it off me!" He flung the covers aside and pulled at the poultice on his foot.

Babe's anger at herself made her growl. "Hush up, you're not taking it off, you hear?"

Rivius pulled frantically at the wrappings on his foot.

Mr. and Mrs. Shaw were on their way upstairs when Babe whispered, "All right, all right, I'll take it off." In the half-light, she was fumbling at the pins that held the bandage when Mr. Shaw lit the lamp.

"Oh my, oh dear," Mrs. Shaw said. The Shaws looked strange in their nightclothes, their hair all awry. Mrs. Shaw bent and put her hand to Rivius' forehead. "Oh, he's hot as a stove," she cried. "Oh, Simon."

"Now, Mama," Mr. Shaw said.

Mr. Shaw picked Rivius up and carried him downstairs. Babe followed and sat beside him on the daybed. She felt afraid of Rivius because he was so sick. She watched the Shaws bumbling about, getting into each other's way and hated them because they had their own safe children. They didn't have to worry about Rivius — she did. She tried to close off all of her feelings.

Mr. Shaw had pulled on trousers over his nightshirt. He had put on his shoes and was struggling into his coat. Mrs. Shaw held his hat.

"I'll tell Gran'ma," Mr. Shaw said, "then I'll hitch Topsy. Don't worry, Mama, don't worry." He did not sound convincing, Babe thought. He paused in the doorway and held the door as though he were waiting for Sprig to follow him.

"I don't believe Sprig ever came back in," Mrs. Shaw said and Mr. Shaw went on out. It was so bright out now that the lamplight inside the house looked feeble.

When old Mrs. Shaw came around, she looked at Rivius and said to Babe, "Simon's gone for Dr. Meade. We'll soon have your brother right as rain again."

"Why does he have to have the doctor?" Babe said. She didn't know why she said that — maybe because she wanted the Shaws to know that she didn't want them to feel put upon — maybe to make them think that she and Rivius and Florence could manage — or maybe so that the old woman would see for sure that this was past Babe's managing.

The old woman turned away without saying anything. She put more cobs onto the fire and filled a kettle from a pail on the stove. Then she said, "Elner, why don't you dress

John and take him and Babe round my side and keep all the children over there?"

Babe moved to get off the daybed. Rivius opened his eyes and said, "Ba-abe." When the grandmother went over to soothe his shoulder, he struck her and said, "I don't want you, I want Babe."

Through the window, Babe could see Shaws' mare coming along the lane. Mr. Shaw pulled Topsy up and he and the doctor got out of the buggy.

Rivius ground his head against the old homespun cover on the daybed, crying loudly as Mr. Shaw and the doctor came in. "I don't like anything," Rivius cried. Babe nodded.

When Mr. Shaw had taken the doctor's coat, he said, "I'm going down to mill."

After he left, Mrs. Shaw said, "Simon'll run the mill empty."

The doctor nodded and asked for a chair. Babe watched with wide eyes as he placed a pad on the chair. On the pad, he placed a lancet and a little cone. He took a bottle and some cotton from his bag and placed those on the chair and asked for a basin. Then he looked at Babe and frowned.

"I'm staying here," Babe growled. The words left her throat feeling raw. It was all she could do to keep from begging out loud, "Don't let me, don't let me." As the doctor went on with his preparations and the old grandmother got a basin, Babe saw that they meant to let her have her way.

The doctor set the chair close to the daybed and drew up another one to sit on. He was so fat, Babe noticed. He uncorked the bottle and poured some of the clear liquid onto a bit of cotton. A sweetish odor floated in the air and Babe

thought she would be sick. She longed to be sick — then they
would have to make her leave. The doctor dropped the
cotton into the little cone and Rivius raised up to see what
he was doing.

"Now, Sonny," the doctor said, "you'll go to sleep and
when you wake up, you'll be better."

Rivius cried, "Get that pewy stuff away from me!" when
old Mrs. Shaw tried to hold the cone over his nose and
mouth. He fought like a wild monkey and Babe thought
her head would split from his screams. Mrs. Shaw told her
to hold his arms and only her anger at the old woman and
at the doctor gave Babe the strength to do it.

Chapter 20

Rivius woke and said to Babe, "You're not allowed
to get off of here. Sit by me."

"I am sitting," she said. "I've sat for an hour or more."

"Huh-uh," he said and squirmed comfortably back to
sleep with his cheek pillowed on his hands.

The doctor had lanced and bandaged Rivius' foot and
given old Mrs. Shaw instructions for caring for it. "I don't
think you'll have any more trouble, Alice," he said.

"The child will be on the road sooner rather than later,
most likely," Mrs. Shaw said in low tones in the doorway.

Babe saw the rueful look on the doctor's face. He shrugged
and said, "Well, I'd say the worst is over. Give the man

instructions to soak the boy's foot—to keep it clean and cover the wound.

"I'm off down to mill now to tell Simon the operation is over and that he can come back to the house. I believe you babied him too much, Alice."

"He's a soft-hearted one all right," Mrs. Shaw said.

Babe sat twiddling her thumbs and thinking that it would be a lot better for Rivius to stay with soft-hearted Mr. Shaw than to go with Mr. Garber. Shouldn't she tell that to the old woman? She could not very well get into the subject, though, without telling things about herself and about Mama and Mr. Garber—shameful things.

After a bit, Babe focused her mind on finding an opportunity to escape to Waterford. In broad daylight, it was going to be a lot harder.

Long before it was dinnertime, Rivius opened his eyes and said, "Babe, I'm hungry—fix me bread and brown sugar." All of the Shaws flocked around to admire how well he looked. Mrs. Elner fixed him a slab of bread and butter and brown sugar but before she and old Mrs. Shaw had gotten the noon dinner on the table, Rivius was inching off the daybed. "My foot doesn't even hurt. I can even step on it, see?" he said.

Old Mrs. Shaw shook her head and smiled, saying, "Children snap in and out of ailments as though they were India rubber balls."

"Is Sprig out catching rats?" Rivius asked Mr. Shaw.

Mr. Shaw said, "I don't know. He may be after a fox. Something got into Gran'ma's chicken coop and Biddy and Min and Duchess are missing. Everything was askew when

Gran'ma went to gather eggs. Sprig was barking in the night. Maybe he's on the fox's trail."

"A fox may have taken Biddy and Min," old Mrs. Shaw said, "but I'll warrant he didn't take Duchess. She's smarter than any fox ever thought of being."

Mr. Shaw took the clock down from the shelf in the front room and laid it on its back on some newspapers on the floor. He began to take its face off.

"What are you doing?' Rivius asked, crawling over to kneel beside Mr. Shaw. "Is that how a clock looks like inside? What's in that cup?"

"It's light oil. I'm going to dip this feather in it and oil the clock. First I have to take it apart and I daren't lose any of its pieces. You can help me keep track of them. When we're finished, we'll go out and whistle up old Sprig."

Rivius gave an ear-splitting whistle.

"Whew," Mr. Shaw said, "that'll bring him, sure."

Babe stayed for the meal. It was not very likely that she could get herself established at anyone's house before this time tomorrow. She might as well eat It was only four or five miles to Waterford. She would beg off from doing the dishes, though. She would say she had to go to the outhouse. By the time they realized that she was gone, she would be well up the road.

As Babe walked along the high sidewalk, she noticed that one of the Shaws' rowboats had come untied and was bobbing on the far side of the race. She wondered how they would fetch it.

On the back of the outhouse door was a calendar picturing a mother with marcelled hair holding a baby. Babe glanced at it and thought of how her own hair was so much like Mama's. She hoped that once she was away from Rivius and Florence she wouldn't think of Mama anymore.

As she let herself out of the outhouse, Babe glanced back at Shaws' house. The part where old Mrs. Shaw lived was low and cozy. Babe thought about the dresser that stood in front of the door between Shaws' front room and old Mrs. Shaw's part of the house. Old Mrs. Shaw kept her privacy. Babe was reminded of her chestnut tree back home.

Some high thin clouds had begun to form in the west. Babe kept encouraging prattle going on inside her head as she jumped off the end of the sidewalk into the chicken yard. An old rooster cast a wing down and strutted around a hen as though it were spring instead of fall. Babe let herself out and redid the fastening of the gate. She'd keep to the tall weeds as much as possible until she came to the road, she decided. She didn't see more than a nettle or two. Mostly, the weeds were pokeweed and dock and goldenrod going brown. It wasn't too far to the road. She could see the line of willows — their wands were a bright yellow.

Babe almost stepped on Sprig. "Ohhh," she said with the back of her hand pressed against her mouth. She was sure the dog was dead, he lay so still. The weeds around Sprig didn't even rustle. Babe glanced back at Shaws' house. Inside, they were tidying up after the meal. Mr. Shaw was letting Rivius and John help him oil the clock. Mr. Shaw was soft-hearted. And here his dog was dead.

Babe decided that she should tell the Shaws. All the way back to the house, she was certain of that. She didn't have second thoughts until she was in the kitchen.

"Babe!" Mrs. Elner said.

Everyone looked up. Babe held her hands out, palms up, as though she were apologizing and said, "I found your dog." She was nonplussed to realize that she hadn't told them Sprig was dead — maybe he wasn't. Maybe she had made a mistake.

Babe looked at one face after the other. All the Shaws had those same blue eyes. Mr. Shaw seemed to guess that Sprig was dead. He ushered Babe out onto the porch before anybody had a chance to say anything. She heard Rivius ask, "Can I go . . ." but then the door closed. Babe led the way with Mr. Shaw following. She didn't think about there being an easier way to get there than to jump down into the chicken yard and go out through the gate.

Mr. Shaw picked Sprig up and held him against his chest. Babe followed him back to the house but this time, they angled over and walked along the wagon lane.

The grandmother had a rock with a dished-out place where it was convenient to lay a nut while you hit it with the hammer. Florence and Isobel and Babe took turns cracking butternuts while Mr. Shaw worked in the kitchen making a box for Sprig. Babe didn't see how he could stand Rivius' questions and remarks.

Mr. Shaw took Sprig's pillow off the rocker and laid it in the box. He carried the dog in from the porch and placed him on the pillow. Then he put the lid he had made in place and nailed it down. Last, he took a pencil from his pocket.

"Write *Sprig*," Rivius said. "Say he was your dog and he was my dog." Babe turned away from the sight of Mr. Shaw crying.

* * *

The butternut cake Isobel's mother made filled the house with the smell of sweetness. Florence and Isobel were cutting "fashions" out of a catalog and lining them up along the carpet. Babe took the *Sunday Dispatch Herald* from the footstool. When she sat to look at it, the word *Sunday* seemed to jump out at her. It wouldn't have done a particle of good to try to find a mailman today — they didn't make their rounds on Sunday. She could have tried to find a place to live and work, though.

A knock on the door startled her. She had begun to be at ease with Mr. Garber's not coming. Now, she had let herself be trapped — she knew it!

Isobel whispered loudly, "Oh, for heaven's sake, it's that picayunish Little Billy. What does he want?"

"Isobel, mind your manners," her grandmother said as Isobel opened the door.

"Yes, what?" Isobel said and Babe slumped in relief behind the paper.

"Isobel," Little Billy said, "no school tomorrow. I came all the way down here to let you know. The schoolhouse is a *mess*. Teacher says it won't be usable in a month of Sundays. She and I just idled down past the schoolhouse after dinner because she was of a mind to get some things she needed and what do we find? Before we was halfway into the yard, I noticed a window was busted."

Little Billy looked past Isobel and said, "Hi, Mrs. Shaw. Hello, Mrs. Shaw. Nice day."

Mrs. Elner Shaw said, "Isobel, invite William in."

Babe looked around the edge of the newspaper and saw Isobel roll her eyes. Little Billy came inside. He was fat and

133

soft looking. "You got company?" he asked, pulling off his blue and orange cap.

"Yes, we have," Isobel said curtly. "Why isn't there any school tomorrow?"

"It was tramps off the railroad — I figured that out right off the bat. When me and teacher got inside the building, you know what we saw?"

"No," Isobel said.

"Well, you wouldn't guess in a hundred years anyway so I'll tell you — it was chicken feathers. There was chicken feathers strewed all around till you would have thought it had snowed. Tramps had got in, wrung some chickens' necks, plucked them, and stewed them up in our drink pail. And there was chicken innards on teacher's desk."

"Little *Billy!*" Isobel said in warning.

"Well, I'm just telling you. I can't help it if that's what I saw. You asked me why there's no school tomorrow and I'm telling you. And you know what they used for plates?"

"What did they use?" Rivius asked.

"Our slates!" Little Billy said triumphantly. "Mine didn't happen to be one of them but I believe yours was, Isobel. Don't you sit second seat, second row?"

"You know where I sit."

"Well, you'll see your slate greased with chicken fat and there's a pile of bones in your pencil slot. I'm not lying."

"Is your mama going down there to help clean up?" Mrs. Elner Shaw asked.

"Oh, yes," Little Billy said. "Being's teacher boards at our place, we feel it's more or less of our duty."

"Why, Gran'ma and I could go down and lend a hand in the morning," Mrs. Shaw offered.

134

"Indeed we could," old Mrs. Shaw said. "I hate to see the schoolhouse out of circulation."

Mrs. Elner Shaw said suddenly, "But Gran'ma, what if the children's . . . You know . . . Someone should be here . . ."

The old woman folded her lips. "Well, we'll see," she said to Little Billy. "You can notify your mother and the teacher that at least one of us Shaw women will be down there first thing in the morning. We'll bring our own scrubbing supplies. Mr. Shaw will set a new light in the broken window, too. That oughtn't to be let go. He's down to mill now but I'll tell him. Most likely he's got a pane of glass in the mill or shed that would do. He'll attend to it."

When Isobel had closed the door on Little Billy, she said to Florence, "Oh, he gets my goat something awful." Then she turned to her mother. "Mama, that's terrible about the schoolhouse. I was hoping that if Florence and Babe and Rivius' papa didn't come, they could go to school with me for the day tomorrow."

Monday, October 8, 1906

Chapter 21

Babe woke with a start. Dread gripped her so strongly that she imagined she was crying out. She was awake enough to know that she was lying in Isobel's bed beside Rivius and that the window across the room was still dark and that that was important. I must have had a bad dream, she told herself. This was the morning she was going off on her own — she should be glad about it. The darkness was getting a worn-out look to it. It was time.

Babe eased from the bed and straightened her clothing before pulling into Isobel's old coat. Then she picked up her shoes, concentrating fiercely on being quiet. Breathing in perfect silence, she crossed to the stairs. She waited on each step while her heart drummed she didn't know how many beats. The same with the door latches. Trying to be so quiet kept her from thinking about leaving Florence and Rivius.

Babe was glad that there was no Sprig to give her away. All of the Shaws and Florence had wept at his burial yesterday. Rivius had clung to Babe's hand, staring in alarm first at Mr. Shaw and then at Babe. Babe was dry-eyed. She hadn't been able to cry for a long time, it seemed to her. She supposed Shaws thought she wasn't sorry about Sprig. She didn't like Sprig, but just the same, she was sorry because he was dead.

Babe sat in the half-dark on the porch step, jamming her

feet into her shoes. She peered around through the gloom. She had gotten into the habit of being on the lookout for Mr. Garber although she didn't expect to see him now. Since he had let this much time pass before coming back to get them, Babe decided that he had gone off someplace on a binge or maybe back to Union. He needed Shorty Spence and Mr. and Mrs. Crowley — he didn't need her and Florence and Rivius. They were only a trial to him. Or maybe he'd gone off elsewhere with that Link . . . Babe shuddered. Shaws' sidewalk seemed to disappear into the mist that rolled off the race. Mr. Garber had disappeared, too, Babe thought. She was glad.

Babe started along the wagon lane through swatches of fog. She felt brief anger at Mr. Garber for just dumping them on Shaws but it worked out well this way. If she hadn't had Shaws to look after Florence and Rivius, she might not have been able to make herself leave. Mad as she had been at Rivius and Florence for being part of Mama's tangled life, she didn't want bad things to happen to them. The anger was gone, she guessed. No, it wasn't — it was just covered up and sore, the way the splinter had been in Rivius' foot.

Babe turned onto the road. She didn't feel like running. The weather was too muggy. If she ran, she would get sweated and she wouldn't look presentable. Besides, she wanted to come across a mailman and a mailman wouldn't be out on his rounds at this hour.

Dorey Peterson, Dorey or George. William was already dead and gone according to the letter in Babe's pocket. Who was to say Dorey and George wouldn't be dead, too, after seven long years. She almost wished they were. Babe decided that the thought of finding out about Mama and about her own father was what had filled her with dread this morning. She wanted to forget them and start a new life for herself. Babe looked behind her, measuring how far she had come away from Rivius and Florence — and from Mama — and from Mr. Garber. The distance back to Shaws' lane didn't look very important.

As she walked along, Babe glimpsed cows clustered at pasture gates, their bags heavy with milk. The reedy crows of roosters were muffled by the thickness of the air this morning. The lighter it got, the less promising the day looked but Babe couldn't make herself care about the weather.

She began to wonder if she had forgotten something. She bit her lip, trying to think. In a moment, she decided she was being silly. What was there to remember? She was dressed decently. All she had had to come away with were Mama's letter and Isobel's buttonhook.

At first Babe had thought Isobel was a big baby and she couldn't wait to get away from her any more than she could wait to get away from Rivius and Florence. Now, she felt a twinge, thinking how generous Isobel had been with her things. Isobel tried to care what people thought and tried to care about how they felt — well, except for that Little Billy. Babe frowned a little as she pictured the chicken mess that Little Billy had described. She fingered Isobel's buttonhook. Isobel and Florence would be friends . . . if Florence stayed at Shaws' . . . Well, she *would* stay at Shaws'. Mr. Garber didn't give two whoopees about her. He was glad to be shut of all of them, Babe told herself.

A blue racer ran for weeds just ahead of Babe and she squealed and stood still, pulling her hands up tight under her chin. She had the feeling that she and this snake were the only things in the world. At last, she got the courage to inch her arms down. There will always be snakes, she thought. Even though I'll be free and separate and on my own so that I can forget about Mama, there'll still be snakes.

Babe sprinted past the snake place and stopped to wipe cobwebs from her face. The willows lining the road were so immense that their wands tangled overhead. Mama always told them not to climb willows. She said you couldn't trust willow wood. A chestnut was different. Even lightning-struck . . . With a pang, Babe thought of Jeroo stuck in the chestnut back home. It was Mr. Garber's fault that she had left Jeroo. A lot of things were his fault. Babe hated him as much as she did Mama but it didn't hurt at all to hate him—he was mean—he did mean things. She was surprised that she hadn't hated him all these years. She hadn't, she decided, because she was used to him. Besides, all of them had Mama, so it didn't really matter.

Babe turned to thoughts of her own father. She wanted to hate him but there wasn't much way to go about hating somebody you'd never heard of until five days back. But, he'd left her and Mama, hadn't he? Suppose, though, it was the other way around and Mama had left him. She wouldn't have. Even if Babe's father had been as mean as Mr. Garber, Mama would have stayed. It was clear to Babe that her father was the one who was at fault. Suddenly Babe snorted. Nothing was clear and she would never rest easy until she found out the whys and wherefores. To do that, she had to find the Petersons.

Slyly, Babe opened the next mailbox she came to, to make

sure she hadn't somehow missed the mailman. Satisfied, she walked on.

As she continued past farms, Babe sighed. It wasn't going to be easy to find a place to live and work. She had only been pretending it would. She'd give her eyeteeth to be settled in someplace right this minute. It was going to storm.

The morning was so gloomy that she almost missed the mailman. A distance ahead was a crossroads. A little mare and buggy came trotting from the road off to the right. After the turn, they continued on a bit before pausing at a mailbox.

"Eww!" Babe cried. She didn't waste breath calling, only ran as fast as she could. When she caught up to the buggy, her throat was too dry to speak.

" 'Morning," the mail carrier said. "Who do we have here?" Without waiting for Babe to answer, he glanced at the sky and said, "Not a very good morning, is it? We may be in for a drenching." He was a slight old man, his Adam's apple jagged as a rock shard.

"Do you . . . ? Do you by any chance know where some Petersons live? I have an address—R.F.D. 5, Waterford."

The mail carrier went on sorting newspapers and letters on the seat beside him but in a moment he said, "Just a awful sad thing." The mare stomped and blew and he said, "Now there, Star, hold up, just hold up."

"Do you know where Petersons live?" Babe asked again.

"Well, I reckon I do."

"Is it anywhere close around here?"

"I reckon it is. If you want to be brung there, I can bring you. I go right past. Hop up.

"Ain't relations, are you?" the mailman asked as Babe climbed into the buggy.

Babe shook her head. "I'm going to work there," she said.

"So Zelda Peterson's got over thinking she can do everything single-handed without 'ary a bit of help. She's just let that place go to seed and I bet Dorey takes that awful hard. I wisht you could have seen the Peterson place in its heyday — it was a sight, I'll tell you. Flowers, flowers, flowers. Oh my, the flowers.

"All righty, Star, there's a good girl, off we go."

Almost at once, the mare turned up a steep lane. "See that?" the mailman said. "Turns right in of her own accord. If I's to die in my tracks, Star could deliver the mail herself. It don't take more'n a minute to take the mail up to Nell Gregory. She's got her hands full — a flock of little childern and her old mother besides. If you look, you can see the old lady settin' by the window. She don't lift a finger, she just sets. Declared when her man passed away that her life's work was done. She's been true to her word — she ain't lifted a finger since. Nell does for her. I figure the least I can do to lighten Nell's load is to trot the mail up to her so she don't have that long trek down to the box. I won't be a minute. Set tight."

Babe thought about the lie she had told the mailman and wondered who Zelda Peterson was. That name had not been in Mama's letter.

A sudden gust of wind blew a flock of didies off a hedge where they had been spread to dry. Just as suddenly, a half-grown kitten tackled one of the didies. He was black with white boots on his feet. Once Florence had had a little cat like that.

144

When Eddie Fetzer was born, Fetzers sent word to Mama asking if she would work for them for a spell — they would pay her in milk and butter and cheese. Babe and Florence ran home, pushing and shoving each other with excitement over the idea. When they told Mama, though, she said, "No . . . They have a lot of folks in and out over to Fetzers' . . . I don't believe I will."

Babe and Florence had been crestfallen. Even when Babe pointed out to Mama that she could watch Fetzers' cows whenever she took the notion if she was working over there, Mama said no, she guessed she wouldn't. When Babe and Florence told Mrs. Fetzer the next day that Mama couldn't come, they volunteered to take her place. They thought it would be nice to see all Fetzers' company and dandle their new baby. Turned out, Mrs. Fetzer set them to washing milk pans. They got tired of it in a minute and Florence squatted in the doorway of the milkhouse playing with Fetzers' kittens. Babe struggled on for a little bit, mostly wiping the water that kept dripping off her elbows. When Mr. Fetzer came up with the milk, he told them to run on home, they were too small. "Want a kitty? Take one, each of you," he had called after them.

Babe had shaken her head. She was aggravated over the way the job had turned out. Florence had exclaimed with pleasure. "Oh, this one . . . No, this. You little precious," she had cooed, picking up first one kitten, then another.

"Pick one," Babe had ordered. "Hurry up."

"Which one do you think?" Florence asked.

"I don't care. Don't take all night." At last Babe said, "How about the black one with the white boots on his feet?"

"Yeah," Florence said gratefully, picking up the little cat

and holding it close, stroking it with her chin.

Florence didn't have the kitty very long. It got under Mr. Garber's feet and he swore he would wring its neck. Shortly it came up missing and Babe expected that was what happened to it.

Babe's eyes darted over the Gregorys' yard, not seeing anything but the truth of a thought that had come over her. *It was Mr. Garber who had killed Sprig. He was back.* He had come back and prowled around Shaws' in the night and he had killed Sprig for barking at him. Pictures tumbled through Babe's mind: Shaws' boat turned loose, Sprig dead in the weeds . . . and the schoolhouse. She could see Mr. Garber as clear as clear — him and that Link — feasting on stolen chickens. A wave of sickness swept over Babe. She should have told old Mrs. Shaw to get the gun if Mr. Garber and Link came back for Florence and Rivius. Now it was too late.

Chapter 22

Babe watched lightning stab deep into a pasture on the hillside. She hardly heard the thunder. She had *known* Mr. Garber was back! She had known it all last night and this morning but she hadn't *seen* it, she had been concentrating so hard on those blamed Petersons.

As the mailman got back into the buggy, he handed Babe a picture post card. "There now, will you look at that? That's a pitcher of the doings up at Lily Dale. Maudie

Rutherford's gran'ma goes there every season and sends her pitchers back. Oh, I wisht you could see the postals Maudie's got saved up. She's got 'em in albums, neat as a pin. She's got pitchers of Niagra Falls even, and valentines. She's got pitchers of a cyclone out Franklin way and the damage it did. Families are standing around looking over what's left and their names of who they are are printed right there on the postal. I don't know as I'd care for that. I hope we ain't in for a cyclone."

Sheet lightning flickered at the horizon. Overhead, the lower clouds, dirty as rags, ran one way and aloft, clouds ran the other. The post card shook in Babe's hand. She laid it back on the buggy seat without looking at it. What would Mr. Garber do with Rivius and Florence? Where would he take them? How could she find them?

"Now I ain't but two-three more deliveries and then I'll drop you off to Petersons and Star and I'll head for home." The mailman glanced behind them and pointed. "Look at that sky, low there. She's raining to a fare-thee-well down French Creek way. Well, we'd best hump."

They had not gone far when the mailman said, "There's your place down yonder there. Used to was, that was a regular showplace.

"Pitiful thing . . . See round down behind? That building? Looks to be fallin' down? Well, it ain't fallin' down — that's as far as it ever got built up. The young feller was working on it. Roof beam fell. Struck him. Just one of those things. His hour was up, that's all — that's the way I look at it. Not Will Peterson though — that was his pa — nope, not him." The mailman paused to batten down things in the buggy.

"Will doted on the boy too much — his mother did, too, for that matter. Likely, if the older folks had let the youngsters go their own way instead of everlastingly trying to tell them what to do, that accident wouldn't have happened." The wind skirled dried willow leaves and overhead the willow whips stood straight out to the west, combed neat as hair. "Stands to reason — if Dorey and Will had let George and little Annamae go off on their own once they was married and had their little baby . . . Stands to reason a young girl wants a place of her own. My daughter was the same way. 'Course, Annamae nor George neither was dry behind the ears yet, but I've seen the young take holt and do. Will blamed Annamae for what happened but come down to it, George was as anxious as she was to get out from under his folks' thumbs. Will never got over it. Dorey, she stayed on at the home place till she was took bad here a few years back. Will's sister come to do for her."

Babe's head had gone woozy. She could only see in a tunnel along the brown line of the mare's back. Her vision stopped altogether with the black prick of the mare's ears.

"Well, you hop out now and run before you get rained on. Good luck to you."

Babe took shelter in a stand of lilac bushes and stared at Petersons' house. There was a porch along the front and around the side. At one end of the side porch, warm yellow lamplight came through the window. She knew that Dorey Peterson was her grandmother! Babe took a few steps toward the house. The wind snatched at her skirts and she fought them back into place. The *George* in the letter was her father. He had been working on a house for Mama and him . . . and her. From where she was, Babe could not see the unfinished building. She stopped, overwhelmed with sadness.

Lightning flashed and the thunder that followed was so strong she could feel it in her jaws. Alarm made her duck back into the cluster of lilacs. She looked out at the house, weathered gray, and imagined Mama walking on the porch, maybe even carrying her as a baby or sitting on the steps with her. Babe felt as though she were seeing ghosts. When the thunder let up, she would run up to the house. Dorey Peterson would be able to tell her all the things she had missed knowing all these years — things she had been cheated out of knowing because she had always thought that Mr. Garber was her father. It was past understanding that Mama had allowed her to believe that. But Dorey Peterson had known Mama and known her the way Babe wanted Mama to *be*.

Babe eyed the safe lamplight as she thought about Dorey Peterson. The only picture of her that she could conjure up reminded her of Isobel's grandmother. But Babe decided that Dorey Peterson was a lot different from Mrs. Shaw. If she hadn't been, she would never have let someone blame Mama for something that wasn't her fault. How could William Peterson blame Mama for what happened! It *wasn't* Mama's fault. It was just one of those things. It wasn't anybody's fault.

Suddenly Babe thought of Rivius and Florence. Old Mrs. Shaw wouldn't let Mr. Garber and Link Roche take them, she promised herself. Then she remembered that Mrs. Shaw had told Little Billy that one of the Shaw women would go down this morning to help clean up the schoolhouse.

What if old Mrs. Shaw was the one who went? What if only Isobel's mother was there when Mr. Garber came?

Chapter 23

Babe decided to go back to Shaws'. When she gained the road, she gasped to see the clouds boiling over the horizon ahead. She would be struck as sure as shooting, she thought. She was so scared her legs wouldn't work right. Her knees jerked up and down crazily. Frantic, she ran up into an orchard alongside the road. That seemed a safer place than out in the open.

As she struggled over the uneven ground, Babe remembered that Mrs. Brown had called her come-by-chance. *I'm not any such!* Babe thought. She tripped and weed stubble sliced up under the skin of her knee. Then she was up and running again.

Pictures of Mr. Garber and Link Roche taking Rivius and Florence from Mrs. Elner Shaw drove Babe down into the road where she could run faster. The wind had swept the road clean of dust and the stones stood up like warts so that it was easy to avoid them. If she could just get back to Shaws' in time . . .

Blinding lightning stopped Babe in her tracks. When the thunder ended, she was bathed in sweat. She longed desperately to be where there were feather pillows — where she could get up onto a table and be safe. There seemed to be a sudden indrawn breath and rain came down in sheets. Seconds later, glassy marbles of hail bounced.

"Ow!" Babe cried. She covered her head with her hands and ran for a thicket at the road's edge and burrowed into it.

When the hail eased off, she crawled out and ran again, snorting and spitting rain. *Get the rifle, get the rifle, get the rifle* . . . Except for the drum of those words, she felt as though she were asleep inside her own head.

As she neared the turnoff to the mill, Babe grew aware that the water was getting so deep that it half covered her shoes. Water was everywhere and it occurred to her that the race had overflowed its banks the way Isobel said it sometimes did. Small sticks began to ride current past her ankles. As she waded for Shaws' porch, Babe saw Duchess teetering on the fence in front of old Mrs. Shaw's garden. Duchess' scrawny neck showed through her wet feathers.

Babe scrambled onto the porch and hugged the wall of the house, blowing to get her breath and trying to wring her clothes and hair. All this water about, and her gullet was as dry as dust.

When she had her breath, she stumbled over to pound on Shaws' door. Old Mrs. Shaw opened the door almost at once. "Babe!" she cried. "Oh, child, where have you been? We've been out of our heads with worry!" She drew Babe inside the house and shut the door. "Look at you, soaked to the hilt!"

Suddenly, wet as Babe was, the old woman hugged her. Then, before Babe could open her mouth, old Mrs. Shaw hurried to the stove and stooped to the cob basket.

"Where are they?" Babe cried, her voice hoarse with worry.

"Did he come? Was that other man still with him?" Babe took the old woman's arm to hamper her and make her listen.

"Who?" Mrs. Shaw asked.

"Rivius and Florence. Where are they?" The house sounds were still except for the purr of the fire and the rain against the windows. Babe knew Florence and Rivius were gone. She dreaded Mrs. Shaw's answer.

"Why, Simon's taken the whole caboodle down to Caroline's. Her place is a good deal farther from French Creek and her land lies higher than ours. French Creek's on a rampage and we were heartsick over you. Where were you? What possessed you to leave that way? Florence was that downhearted — Rivius, too — not to mention the rest of us.

"Out of your wet things. Make a heap of them. Here are dry towels. We'll forgo the bath — too much water about as it is. We won't add to it. I wouldn't wonder the water will come in the house this time." She went to the window and rubbed it with the dishcloth so that she could peer out.

Babe was grateful for the old woman's turned back. Mrs. Shaw kept looking out the window a good deal longer than it took her to discover that she couldn't see anything past the rain.

Babe yanked out of her wet clothing. "Are you sure Rivius and Florence are with Mrs. Elner and Isobel and them?"

"Well, of course I'm sure. Where else would they be?" When Mrs. Shaw turned around, Babe was wrapped in a towel, shivering and trying to part her hair with her fingers. "Stand tight to the stove while I go up and get dry things."

The old woman wasn't halfway up the stairs when Babe called, "When did they leave?"

"About noon, I suppose—I don't know—when the weather worsened."

Babe called, "You don't think anything would have happened to them on the way, do you?"

Mrs. Shaw came to the top of the steps and started down with dry clothing over her arm. "Of course I don't think anything happened to them. I'll warrant they're safe and sound at Aunt Caroline's right this minute. Most likely that little Rivius has everyone in stitches with his didoes. Simon'll be along back any time now and tell you himself that he delivered everybody safely. There's still a good deal of battening down to do around here and the stock to tend to.

"Here, dress warmly. The kettle's boiling. I'll make us something hot to warm our stomachs."

As Babe pulled into Isobel's clothing, she asked, "Did . . ." She could not bring herself to say Mr. Garber's name. Finally she said, "Did anybody come looking for Rivius and Florence?"

"Why no, not your papa, if that's who you mean."

"He isn't my papa," Babe said in a low voice. She wasn't even sure that the old woman would hear her above the rain but Mrs. Shaw looked around sharply.

"Why, I thought . . ." She held a handful of rolled oats over the steaming kettle.

"He's Rivius' and Florence's papa," Babe said miserably. She was surprised that Mrs. Shaw did not say anything. She dribbled the oats into the boiling water, stirring. Babe finished buttoning Isobel's dress and tied the sash.

"Oatmeal makes sturdy eating—good for man and beast alike," the old woman said.

Babe took two bowls from the cabinet.

"Get the brown sugar for sweetening," Mrs. Shaw said, "and there's cream in the pitcher."

As they ate, Babe said, "Do you think the water outside is getting pretty deep?"

"I don't know but I expect so. Floods don't alarm me. The worst is the mess they leave. I've cleaned up after many a one in my time and I suppose I'll clean up after many a one more. Right now, I want us to be fortified in peace. I still feel gratefulness abuilding that you've come back and that you're safe."

Babe dug a ditch through the oatmeal and watched the cream run into it. She had the same feeling about Rivius and Florence's being safe as Mrs. Shaw did about her. The thought struck her, though, that with Mr. Garber still around, they were not safe. When she glanced up at the old woman, Babe changed her mind again. Mrs. Shaw would get the rifle.

Babe said, "I didn't want to be here . . ." She took a deep breath and started again. "I didn't want to be here when Mr. Garber came." The old woman did not look up from her oatmeal. Wind gusted down the chimney, making smoke belly out of the stove. "I didn't leave just on account of him and Link Roche, though," Babe said. "I left on account of Rivius and Florence, too."

"But you came back on account of Rivius and Florence, didn't you?"

Babe ran her spoon around the bowl, driving grains of oatmeal down into the cream. "I guess so," she said softly. When she looked up, she looked directly into Mrs. Shaw's blue eyes. "Yes," Babe said. "I was afraid that Mr. Garber would

take them. I didn't want him to—I wanted . . ." She left
the rest of the sentence unfinished It would be awkward
saying that she wanted Rivius and Florence to stay at Shaws'.
Besides, the things she wanted didn't come to pass. There was
no use saying them.

"Didn't you know I wouldn't have let them go with him?"
Babe sighed. "Yes, I knew," she said. She stared at her
image in the silver bowl of the spoon. She was upside down.
That was the way with a lot of things, she thought. You
could know for positive about things and yet they seemed
to be just the opposite.

Babe was thinking about Mama when old Mrs. Shaw
asked, "What became of you children's mama?"

"She wasn't Florence's—just Rivius' and mine." Babe
licked the spoon so that she could see herself more clearly
and then said, "No, she was Florence's, too—not her real
mother who was married to Mr. Garber—but she was
Florence's mama just the same." After she stirred her oatmeal a bit, she said, "Mama died—I don't know—one day
this week. Afterwards, Mr. Garber said he was taking us
to Conneaut. I guess he knows someone there."

"Maybe he's gone on to Conneaut."

Babe shook her head. "Huh-uh, he's around here. He
killed Sprig, he took your—Oh!" Babe jumped up. "Duchess
was perched on your fence! I forgot to tell you!"

"Oh, that Duchess!" the old woman cried. She got up from
the table, caught up her shawl from the chairback, and followed Babe.

Outside, Babe was shocked to find that the water was
well up on the porch steps. She saw a snake swimming past,
its head reared—and then another. Some animal with a

black muzzle was clawing to get aboard a good-sized branch carried by the current. Babe walked as close to the porch edge as she dared. She craned to try to see Mrs. Shaw's fence. "Oh, I don't see anything anymore!" she cried.

"My fence may have joined the Allegheny by this time," Mrs. Shaw said. Suddenly, above their heads, there was a squawk and they looked up to see Duchess roosting on a tiny ledge under the eave of the porch roof.

Mrs. Shaw smacked her hands. "Duchess, bless your old heart! Come down, come down here, chick, chick, chick."

The hen tried to stand, shifting her feet and stretching her neck. "You'll fall!" Babe cried.

"No, she won't. She's too smart for that. Come, chick, chick, chick."

"Maybe if she sees you've got some bread for her . . ."

Babe was still struggling with the bread safe when Mrs. Shaw came in with Duchess. The hen had her wet head tucked under Mrs. Shaw's arm.

As Mrs. Shaw toweled the hen, Babe said, "We could make her a spot under the stove. Want me to?" She took another towel and curled it into the shape of a nest and placed it in the warmth under the ash drawer. Then she broke up bread in little pieces and put them on the table so that Mrs. Shaw could offer them to the hen on her lap.

"Silly old spindleshanks," Mrs. Shaw said, smoothing the hen. Duchess ruffed out her feathers and settled them here and there with her beak. Then she began to pick bread from Mrs. Shaw's hand. Babe knelt on the floor, watching. "Boy, she's a one, isn't she?" Babe said, clicking her tongue and nodding her head.

At last Mrs. Shaw got up and placed Duchess in the nest. She brushed crumbs from the table and stood with them cupped in her hand, looking at the clock. She said, "You're back, Babe. Duchess is back. We're only wanting for Simon now. I'll be bound he's slow. We won't worry but I think we should take action here. That water's risen a good deal since two o'clock and there's precious little letup in the rain."

Chapter 24

Babe carried cushions and catalogs and the footstools and two little tables upstairs while Mrs. Shaw put things up off the floor in the kitchen and front room.

"How come you stayed here?" Babe asked suddenly. "How come you didn't go with them?"

"I was anxious about you. I didn't want you to come back to an empty house." After glancing at Babe's rueful face, old Mrs. Shaw said, "Oh, most likely I would have bided anyway—a flood would hardly know how to get on without me."

They rolled the pieces of carpet in Mr. and Mrs. Shaw's bedroom and placed them on the big bed and lifted John's trundle bed up on top of them. Then they took Duchess upstairs and penned her in a box. When they came back down, Babe cried, "Lookit!" Water was seeping under the door and soaking the front room carpet in an ever-widening arc. A mouse ran squeaking from a corner.

"How can we keep the water out?" Babe cried. She

whisked towels from the kitchen and ran to sop at the rug and to press the towels against the bottom of the door. "If we had a board to put here . . ."

"It wouldn't do any good," the old woman said.

"But I don't want the water to slop up everything!" Babe said. "There's got to be a way to stop it!"

Mrs. Shaw said, "Some things can't be dealt with in ways we ordinarily think of. Some things we just have to see beyond. I don't doubt but what the sun will come out again and that down the line there will be clean fresh. Today's a dark day but it won't always be this way. The carpet will dry when the time comes. Now, it's time for you and me to get up out of the water's reach." She stoked the stove with cobs. She placed two chairs on the kitchen table and tucked two quilts and her galoshes under them before she and Babe climbed up.

It was a curious thing, Babe thought, to be sitting in a chair on top of the table next to old Mrs. Shaw. After a bit, she remarked, "My mama and us would take to the kitchen table when it lightened and thundered. We kept our feet on pillows. Feathers keep you from getting struck."

"I've heard that," Mrs. Shaw said. "I think likely it's true. Haven't we Duchess to prove it?"

Babe nodded absently. She was thinking of Petersons.

Watching her, Mrs. Shaw said, "Don't worry, the children are safe. Simon will be along." Babe nodded in the flickering lamplight.

By and by, Babe said, "I know where my own grandmother lives."

"I was wondering if you had folks."

Babe examined that possibility. The only people she really knew were Florence and Rivius and Mama and . . .

"Where does she live?" Mrs. Shaw asked.

"Toward Waterford . . . I was there . . ." Babe stopped in confusion. It didn't seem right to make Mrs. Shaw believe that she had a grandmother whom she knew and who knew her. "It's not like you and Isobel," Babe said hastily. "I don't even know her. I just know where she lives." She was sorry she had spoken of the subject at all. She wished she did not know where Dorey Peterson lived. She wished she'd never read Mama's letter.

At least three mice were swimming or clambering about in the kitchen. "Sprig would have had a grand time," Mrs. Shaw remarked.

"I'm sorry about Sprig," Babe said.

"I know. Dogs come and go. There'll be others. When I was a little girl, we had an old dog, Buster. My, that was many a long year ago now. When I was a youngster, there were still Indians about. Father was a miller in Venango County. He was down to mill one day when a pair of Indians surprised me. They wanted me to take them across the river in our skiff. As luck would have it, Buster was nowhere about — just as well, maybe. Anyhow, if my scalp didn't tingle all the way across that river!" Mrs. Shaw tucked a hairpin in closer. "But as you see, I still have my scalp. When we reached the other bank, the Indians grunted and climbed out and disappeared into the woods. I was nine years old at the time.

"My mother had died early that year and left Father with four of us children. I was the oldest. Mother had taught me to cook and clean and spin and sew and she taught me what little she knew of reading and ciphering so I was well equipped. I mised her sorely, though. I raised my brothers and sister for two years, nearly three, when Father decided to marry again. Wasn't I put out! I never did take to my stepmother. I knew as much as she did, I thought. I left home before I was fourteen to work for a woman. When I got a little money put by, I made my way to Erie. Oh, Erie was some pickings, I thought. I got a job in a hotel, washing dishes."

Babe was trying to think how she really felt about Mama. It still seemed to her as though Mama had wronged her. On the other hand, the Petersons had wronged Mama. If only she knew the ins and outs of it. Struggling to think of something to say, she remarked, "My mama was good at sewing. I know how to sew."

"Did she crochet as well?" Mrs. Shaw asked. Without waiting for an answer, she said, "Land, the happy hours I've spent crocheting. If all the nightie yokes I've made were laid side by each, they'd stretch from here to China. I was four years old and sick abed when Mother first taught me the chain stitch. My, oh my — two years older than John, half as old as Rivius. Can you imagine! My mother was a patient woman if ever there was!"

"I can just picture Rivius with a crochet hook," Babe said. The thought struck her so funny that she began to laugh and couldn't stop until she made herself think about the muddy water inching up around the table legs. At last she said, "My mama was patient, too." She told Mrs. Shaw about the day Mama had set her and Florence to making the Jeroos.

Babe told other things about Mama — about her fondness for cows and her way with flowers. Suddenly she was silent. Until that moment, she had not pieced together Mama's love for flowers and the mail carrier's remark about the Petersons' being a showplace. "... *Flowers, flowers, flowers. Oh my, the flowers.*" There must have been special things between Mama and Mrs. Peterson. Babe had to see Mrs. Peterson after all. She had to talk about Mama.

Abruptly Babe said, "I hope the water's gone down tomorrow. I'm going to my grandmother's house." She felt sweat break out on her palms as she said it.

Mrs. Shaw did not comment at once. After a little bit, she said, "It may be a day or two."

"Till the water goes down?"

"Yes."

"I have to go to my grandmother's as soon as I can." The lamp had about guttered out so that they had only the glow of the stove for light. It glistened on the floating straw that had washed out from under the carpet.

Babe wondered if Dorey Peterson would remember Mama. She wondered if she should tell her who she was — she didn't want to. She was not sure she wanted to go to Petersons' at all. Thinking of it, she began to kick her legs back and forth.

"Floods cultivate patience in a person," Mrs. Shaw said.

"I'm tired of waiting."

"We'll set the chairs down out of the way and you can cover with the quilt here and try to sleep."

"I don't feel like sleeping."

Babe must have slept. When she woke, it was very dark

161

inside the room but she sensed at once that Mrs. Shaw was alert.

"Listen," Mrs. Shaw said. "I want you to stay here. You're awake now so you won't tumble off into the water. For a while I've seen lanterns going to and fro down at the mill. I'm surprised Simon hasn't come for us. I want to go out and see."

"The water's over your galoshes. How can you go out?"

"I have a scheme."

Babe sighed. She sat up and pulled the quilt around her shoulders.

"Will you be all right?" Mrs. Shaw asked.

"I suppose so. I don't see how you're going to get through the water."

"I'll use the chairs — stand on one chair and step across to another. Then I'll swing the first one round in front of me and do the same thing again. First one and then the other. The water isn't more than four or five inches deep in here. I'll go as far as the porch and holler. I can't understand why Simon . . . Well, I'll find out. Will you be all right?"

Babe's only answer was a sniff but when she judged that Mrs. Shaw had reached the porch, she called, "Be careful!"

"Yes. Be patient."

"Puh-h," Babe said softly. She sat with her knees updrawn, watching the window. The rain seemed to have stopped. She decided that it must be almost morning — the darkness didn't seem so black. She heard Mrs. Shaw calling and heard shouts from down by the mill but she couldn't make out what was being said. She watched the lanterns bobbing in the distance for what seemed a long time. Finally she called to Mrs. Shaw. When there was no answer, she thought, *What if she's fallen? What if she needs help?*

With growing alarm, Babe climbed down onto a chair and maneuvered another chair so that she could step across to it. She didn't see how Mrs. Shaw managed — it was so hard to swing the chairs. Hastly, she undid her shoes and pulled off her stockings and left them on one of the chairs. The unpleasant feel of the soaked carpet made her shudder as she crossed the front room and went out onto the porch.

Babe was relieved to be out of the house. Mrs. Shaw's chairs were on the porch but she was gone. Babe struggled against panic when suddenly she heard Mrs. Shaw's voice. She had gone to the mill. From the mill, Babe heard a man's voice, too, crying, "Left, Jack! Shift more to the left! More!" Sounds carried clearly over the expanse of water.

Overhead, the morning star seemed to be caught in the branches of the big sugar maple that grew by the house. Babe decided that if Mrs. Shaw had been able to get to the mill, she could manage, too. She'd hike her skirts up and step high, wide, and handsome. And she'd keep a firm grip on the railing.

As Babe neared the mill, she paused, shivering, to see what was happening. There were three boats clustered at the place where the flume had fed water to the millwheel. Lanterns rocked in two of the boats — the third boat was overturned. The men in the boats had long-handled grappling hooks and ropes. By the light of a lantern hung in the mill doorway, she could see old Mrs. Shaw on the platform. The platform was stacked with sodden bags of grain or flour.

At first Babe thought it was another bag of grain that

the men were fishing out of the muddy water. The rivulets of water that ran from it were golden in the lantern light.

Someone asked, "Do you know who it is, Simon? You, Jack?"

It came to Babe then that it was a man they had struggled to pull out of the water.

Mrs. Shaw had built a roaring fire in the stove in the office. Babe's face flamed with the warmth of it. Her teeth rattled away although she did not feel cold. The man was Mr. Garber, she knew it.

The office had been ransacked. Papers and ledgers from the wall desk lay about the room. Grain was spilled everywhere. Many of the bags of grain from the stack where Sprig liked to sleep were gone.

"That was Mr. Garber," Babe said. Mrs. Shaw looked up from chafing Babe's feet and nodded. "We'd give the world for you not to have seen that," she said.

Babe did not say anything. She had seen it.

Tuesday, Wednesday, Thursday
October 9, 10, 11, 1906

Chapter 25

Hoarfrost fretted the walls of Isobel's bedroom. It had turned sharply cold. Babe lay awake, listening to Duchess churking away in the box nearby. She was thinking about Mr. Garber. She did not know how to feel about his being gone. She thought she should feel glad but she only felt empty and tired. Babe tried to imagine how Mr. and Mrs. Crowley or Shorty Spence would feel. Suddenly she thought of Mrs. Brown. Babe imagined her saying, "Well, Ris Garber, so you've got your comeuppance." That made her so angry that she got up and dressed, her teeth chattering. Babe didn't want to feel the way Mrs. Snoop did — not for more than a hundred dollars.

On Tuesday, Babe and Mrs. Shaw did not accomplish much more than setting the stove to rights. Mrs. Shaw said, "There will be men to feed and goodness knows we need plenty of warmth to dry things out."

Wednesday, Mrs. Elner came home, leaving Isobel and Florence, Rivius and John at Caroline's. Mr. Shaw and three men he had hired from Mill Village began to repair the damage to the dam and the mill. It was up to the two Mrs. Shaws to deal with the house. Babe was anxious to go to Petersons' but she thought that she should stay and help the Shaws. She was astonished at the mess the flood left. She would have thought so much water would have cleaned things instead of messing them. By rights, that's the way things should have been. But they weren't.

As Babe shoveled muck out of corners and plopped it into a pail, she thought about the meeting with Mrs. Peterson. It was going to be so important. It could make a difference in the way she felt about Mama. Maybe it would.

Mrs. Elner pulled her jars of canned fruit out of the bottom of the cupboard and set them in a tub for Babe to wash. "Won't they all be spoiled?" Babe asked. Mrs. Shaw said no, she didn't think so. The jars were in need of washing, that was all — the seals were tight. At noontime, they ate a jar of peaches and they tasted so good.

Toward evening, all three of them were spent. Old Mrs. Shaw said, "I know we've got to quit but if we can just get a cloth on the table, we'll feel human again."

At supper, there was still mud underfoot but Babe placed their plates on a clean cloth.

When Mr. Shaw came in, he had news that Link Roche had been found drowned, too. He was swept partway to Cambridge. Mr. Shaw turned to Babe. "The sheriff was by this afternoon," he said. "As far as he was able to find out, there isn't any reason why you and Florence and Rivius can't stay with us. There's not a thing in the world we'd like better."

"Oh, Babe!" Mrs. Elner cried. As she hugged Babe, a hairpin slithered into Babe's collar and lay cold against her neck. Gran'ma Shaw had her capable hands folded across her apron. Babe glanced at her face and then away. Homely as old Mrs. Shaw was, she was beautiful, Babe thought.

"I have to go to my grandmother's," Babe said softly. She

looked past Mr. and Mrs. Shaw's disappointed faces. Something in old Mrs. Shaw's eyes made Babe know that she was right.

Old Mrs. Shaw walked Babe a little way along the Waterford road. She was of a mind, she said, to see how the little cemetery had fared in the flood. Poor Pa, her husband, was laid there, she said, and her two youngest sons. She spoke gently about them.

Babe did not feel like talking. At first she wished that the Shaws had not let her go. She did not want to leave their place. She was going because she owed it to Mama to try to see clearly the whys and wherefores of her life and Dorey Peterson was the only one who could help her.

At least Florence and Rivius had a safe and happy place to live, Babe thought as she stepped over a piece of willow limb. That was what she had wanted. She couldn't understand why her nose stung with tears. Used to was, if she got what she wanted, she was happy. She guessed it was hard to go away from Rivius and Florence because she was so used to them.

At the cemetery gate, Mrs. Shaw ignored the debris left by the flood. She faced Babe, her old face sober.

"Well, good-bye," Babe said softly.

"Babe," the old woman said, taking both of her hands, "seldom, seldom one comes across a person in this life who *does* the hard thing. Most people don't even see what has to be done, let alone do it." She held Babe close to her bosom for so long that Babe was afraid she would cry.

Babe did not say good-bye again; she turned and walked rapidly toward Waterford. Then she thought to call back to Mrs. Shaw: "Watch out under those willows — willow wood isn't any too trustworthy." Mrs. Shaw nodded her head and waved.

All the way to Petersons' Babe mulled over what she would say when she got there. She couldn't settle on anything. By the time she arrived, she was past worry. If she could get onto the porch and rap on the door . . . If she could manage to do that much . . .

Babe rapped. She held herself stiff as a ramrod. When she heard footsteps inside the house, she swallowed and cleared her throat and cleared it again.

The woman who answered the door opened it only a little bit. It was so dim inside the house that Babe could not see very well. "I'm . . . Is . . ." she stammered. For an instant, she could not remember the name *Peterson*.

"Are you Mrs. Peterson?" she said at last.

"No."

"I wanted to see Mrs. Peterson."

"She's poorly and does not receive."

"But I have to talk to her," Babe said. The woman, who must have been Zelda Peterson, began to close the door. "I'm her granddaughter!" Babe cried.

The word *granddaughter* still rang in her head as the woman stepped out onto the porch and took her by the arm. Zelda reminded Babe of Mrs. Brown.

"Listen here to me," Zelda Peterson said. "I don't know who you are or who put you up to this — those worthless Ameses no doubt. From the time Annamae Ames walked into this house . . . It was Annamae Ames put my brother Will where he is — up to Willis Grove Cemetery. It was Annamae Ames put my sister-in-law Dorey in the position she's in now — a broken woman. We've no time in this house for Ameses so you just *scat!*"

Long after the door had closed in her face, Babe stood with her fists against the door and her heart hammering in her ears. She could not see straight she was so angry.

As Babe walked across the yard, she kept her head high. She didn't hurry one iota. She knew good and well that Zelda Peterson was watching her. Sure enough, the door opened and the woman called, "Go on with you!"

When Babe got to the road, she stopped. In a moment Zelda came out onto the porch and called, "You just go on away from this property. I'll not have you around!"

Babe said, "I intend to wait here. This is a public road and I'll stand here as long as I need to." With that, she turned her back on the woman.

The mailman did not come for a long time. Babe would not let herself believe that she had missed him. All the while she waited, she didn't so much as itch her nose. She knew Zelda Peterson was watching her from behind the lace curtains.

Babe was never so glad to see anything as to see the mailman's little mare approaching. Long before the buggy was close enough, she waved her arms to be sure the mailman would stop.

"Well, well, hello. How are things going? Zelda Peterson keeping you busy? Better weather today, ain't it? You know they was a cloudburst between Wattsburg and Mill Village — French Creek all up out of its banks. They was people drownded in Mill Village. That's too close for comfort. We got off easy with just a tree or two down from the blow."

Babe shaded her eyes from the sun. "Can you tell me where

some folks named Ames live? Do they live around here?"

"Old Ed Ames?"

Babe nodded, relieved that the name was familiar to him.

"Well, Lillian Ames is down to the old place with him, I hear. He ain't good. Maybe it was Lillian you was looking for?"

Babe nodded again. "Either," she said.

"Far as I know, Lillian's been down there . . . oh, a month or more. That old Ed never did a tap for his girls. I'm surprised Lillian's come back now that he's in straits." Suddenly he glanced at Petersons' house. "Working at Petersons', I'm surprised you're looking up the Ameses. There's bad blood between them two families since . . . I mentioned, didn't I, about . . . ?"

"Yes," Babe said, cutting him short. "I just want to know where Ameses live. Are they on your route?"

"Well, they are, but I don't generally stop. They never get any mail and I'm leery of that old man. 'Course, it don't matter now — he's bedfast. I feel sorry for the daughter. Neither of them girls ever had any kind of a life. I don't know what became of Annamae but the older one lived in to Waterford till the old man got down. Then she come back."

"Where, where do they live? Can't you tell me?"

"You planning to go there?"

"I don't know. If you could just tell me . . ."

"Well, if you're set on going . . . It's not that far — maybe three-quarter mile — but that's as the crow flies. It's more like, oh, maybe a mile further by way of the road. They don't have a box but the way in to their place is just beyond a tree that's tied in a knot. Oh, it was before my time. Old Court Taylor — it was his gran'pa tied a knot in a sapling when he was a youngster, just for the devlishness of it. The tree growed that way, can you imagine! Well, I've seen stranger things . . . But anyway, there's a track back in to Ameses'. It ain't much — all overgrowed, so careful you don't miss it."

Babe was in such a hurry to get away from the mail carrier that he had urged Star back to the center of the road before she thought to turn and call, "Thanks, mister."

The mail carrier didn't turn around but raised his hand in a wave.

Chapter 26

Babe trotted along, her footsteps jarring her thoughts. It was queer to think that she had a grandfather. That must be who the old man was — her grandfather. Lillian must be Mama's aunt. No, that wasn't the way of it — she must be Mama's sister and her own aunt.

Babe hardly gave a glance to the tree that was tied in a knot. Making her way back in along the overgrown lane, she had the uneasy feeling that she was back at Garbers'. When she stood at the edge of the yard, a chill came over her arms.

A hard-bitten woman was on the porch, bent over a washboard scrubbing clothes. The washtub was set on a bench next to the wall. "All *right,* Pa, all right," the woman called once. "You just hold your horses till the wash is hung. Then I'll be in."

Babe was not aware that she had crossed the yard. She was standing below the porch when Lillian discovered her. Lillian gave a jump and her wet hand flew to her throat. "Anna-mae," she said.

Before Babe could open her mouth, the woman, her aunt, said, "No, no, it isn't, is it? You must be Georgeanna." The woman came slowly down off the porch and took Babe's shoulders with her wet, soapy hands. "Where's your mama? Oh, you're as like as peas in a pod. Oh, oh . . ." Lillian put her hands up to the sides of her face and her eyes looked on beyond Babe.

An old scarred cat stretched on the porch. He let his neck run out beyond the floorboards and then drew it in again and curled, asleep. Babe could not think what she had done. It was wrong of her to come here. It was clear that Mama had never kept in touch with Lillian. Babe had stirred up trouble, that was all.

"Georgeanna. Little Georgeanna grown big as a . . . Oh, come set. Where's your mama? Oh, I can't believe Anna-mae's mother to a grown-up young lady!" She took Babe's hand and Babe sat by her on the step.

Babe felt as heavy as lead, weighed down by the strange name Georgeanna and by all that she knew of her life and Mama's. She could never tell this woman about it. It didn't matter to her that there were two sides of Mama's life and that she, Babe, had needed to know why. It didn't matter anymore. The only thing she cared about was that she was Babe and belonged to Mama. This woman sitting next to her and smelling of clean lye soap knew her for Mama's and she knew Mama for who she was. None of the rest of it mattered.

From inside the house, the old man called, swearing.

"Hush yourself, Pa. I'll be in when I'll be in," Lillian said. She turned to Babe. "He hasn't changed. You mustn't stay."

Her eyes — the same eyes as Mama's — searched Babe's face. Babe felt desperate. She didn't see how she could keep from talking to Mama's sister.

Lillian's face softened into sorrow. She said, "Annamae's gone, isn't she?" She turned away before Babe had to answer. By and by, Lillian picked up a stick and began to shoo dry leaves with it. She said, "Little Annamae — she had a good deal of grit. I never heard a word of complaint out of her."

The old man shouted and Lillian shouted back, "I told you, Pa, I'll be in when I'll be in." She did not look at Babe, only at the marks she was making in the dirt with the stick as she said, "She left this house at twelve years old and went to work for Dorey and William Peterson. Their boy George took a shine to her. William didn't think Annamae Ames was good enough for him. To my notion — well, no, I hadn't ought to say that. George was all right. It was William Peterson wasn't. William would have had Annamae to go no more than she got there but Dorey liked her. She did stand up to him then. It was when George was killed that she didn't. I haven't forgiven her and oh, Lord, I can't even speak of William Peterson." Lillian's stick sailed through the air.

"Lillian!" the old man called.

"Don't he yap," Lillian said to Babe. She got up and climbed to the porch and began to scrub the clothes again as she talked.

"Annamae came back home with you and tried to live after George was killed. Why, she couldn't even mourn George decent." Lillian jerked her thumb toward the house. When the old man shouted at her again, she stomped inside and Babe heard her shout back at him.

When Lillian came outside, she said, "Annamae was too

gentle. She hadn't the power to give him tit for tat as I do. I was working at a store in Waterford at the time and Annamae tried to do for him and take care of you. Why, she even left off saying your name, trying to suit him. He wouldn't hear the name George under his roof and she tried to suit him. You don't try to suit people like Pa, you . . . Oh . . ." Lillian swung her hand, spattering soapsuds on the cat so that he got up and moved, his tail twitching. "Yes, go on with you," she said to the cat.

"I was at the store and it was there I came across word of someone needing hired help and far enough away from here that . . ."

Babe was not listening. She was struck by how like Mama Lillian wrung clothes — something about the clench of her fingers and the turn of her wrist.

Glass broke around the side of the house. Lillian went to the edge of the porch and said grimly, "Why, he's thrown a cup through the window for spite!"

"I have to go," Babe said. It did not even sound to her as though it was her own voice. She walked halfway up the steps to meet Lillian. She might have leaned a long time against Lillian if she hadn't been frantic to get away. Her head drummed dangerously. She'd felt that way when she was about to puke — unable to think at all.

Ended up, she was sick. Afterwards, she sat up in somebody's orchard on the lee side of an old sweet cherry. She wept and wept, letting the sobs drive her closer and closer to Mama. After that, her head was weak.

Babe didn't think about going back to Shaws', she just went. Rivius and Florence had come back home.

Epilogue: Spring 1907

Chapter 27

Purple flags were in bloom along the edge of the race. A flicker cackled in the woods and a pair of catbirds darted in and out of the hop vine that grew over the chicken coop.

Babe finished raking a flower bed in front of old Mrs. Shaw's part of the house and leaned the rake against the fence. Suddenly she said, "Gran'ma, was Dorey still a one to garden when you would go down to set with Will Peterson?"

Old Mrs. Shaw said, "She was, indeed she was. She could be worn to a nub but when I'd come to spell her, she'd take a turn about the yard, pluck a yellowed leaf here, tie up a posy there. She was a sweet woman. I liked her."

"I wish you could have known Petersons when me and Mama . . . and my father lived there," Babe said. Mrs. Shaw nodded.

Babe picked up a packet of seeds and said, "What do you think, Gran'ma, is this bed smooth enough to plant?"

"It's smooth as silk. Now if we can just keep hens and boys out of it . . ."

Babe knelt on the path that she had swept clean in front of the bed. "How long do you think it will be before they sprout?" she asked, stretching to poke sweet pea seeds into the earth.

Before Mrs. Shaw could reply, Rivius ran shrieking along the lane, with Isobel and Florence chasing him. He jumped onto the garden gate crying, "Help! Gran'ma, Babe, save me!"

Isobel grabbed one of his arms and Florence the other. "Take it back! Say you take it back, Rivius!" they cried.

"Gran'maa!" he cried as the girls pulled at him.

Mrs. Shaw said, "Listen, old featherbritches, woe betide if you break down Babe's and my new gate."

"I won't break it down. If I do, it will be Florence and Izzy to blame."

Isobel said, "Gran'ma, make him take back something he said."

"What did he say?" Babe asked, patting earth over her seeds.

Isobel said, "Oh, I can't stand to repeat it."

"Nor me, neither," Florence said.

Rivius stuck out a foot to fend the girls away and sang,

> *Florence and Izzy are mad and I'm glad*
> *And I know how to please them,*
> *A bottle of ink to make them stink,*
> *And Little Billy to squeeze them!*

Then he screamed with laughter.

Florence cried, "Block your ears, Izzy, block your ears!"

The girls raced around and onto Shaws' porch and slammed inside the house.

Rivius stayed on the gate, squeaking it back and forth. "Gran'ma, he said, "you know what? Papa and me saw Duchess sneaking across the flume."

Mrs. Shaw clicked her tongue. "Well, if that Duchess isn't bound to hide her nest?"

"Will she hatch peeps?"

"I expect so."

"How long will we have to wait?"

"Three weeks is what it takes."

"Oh. Can I come in and see Babe's garden?"

"No!" Babe said. "No boys allowed."

Rivius began to sing, "Babe's mad and I'm glad and . . ."

Babe grinned at him. "Rivius, I think Little Billy is almost as sweet as that little Esther Larkin."

Rivius whined, "Ba-abe." He got off the gate and slipped through it to stand beside Mrs. Shaw. "Gran'ma," he said, "I might quit going to school on account of that Esther. She chases me. Every recess and noontime, she chases me." He rapped himself on the head with his knuckles.

"He loves it, Gran'ma," Babe said.

"I don't!" Rivius cried, stamping his foot.

Babe said, "Your face is turning bright red, Rivius."

Rivius covered his face with his hands. His shoulders shook with laughter.

Mrs. Shaw hugged Rivius to her. " 'In spring, a young man's fancy' . . ." she said.

"I'm going home," Rivius said, pulling away. He let himself out through the gate, latched it, and disappeared around the house. In a few moments he was back. "Hey, Babe, Gran'ma," he said, standing on the gate. "You want to come round our side? The girls are making licklally. Mama says you better set with us for supper, too. She says you must be worn to a frazzle working on that garden."